# Readers love
## Rayna Vause

*Extrasensual Perception*

"It was fun, full of tension, and left me feeling happily warm and fuzzy."

—Love Bytes

"*Extrasensual Perception* was like a bowl of soup on a cold day— comforting and extremely satisfying."

—Joyfully Jay

*Demon of Mine*

"Electrifying and thought provoking, *Demon of Mine* demands and ultimately delivers."

—Joyfully Reviewed

"A fun sweet book about two men who are willing to sacrifice for those they love and fight for a love that has spanned over time."

—Books are love

By RAYNA VAUSE

Demon of Mine
Twice Bitten

DREAMSPUN DESIRES
#26 – Extrasensual Perception

Published by DREAMSPINNER PRESS
www.dreamspinnerpress.com

# Twice Bitten

## RAYNA VAUSE

Published by

DREAMSPINNER PRESS

5032 Capital Circle SW, Suite 2, PMB# 279, Tallahassee, FL 32305-7886 USA
www.dreamspinnerpress.com

Trade Paperback ISBN: 978-1-64080-747-1
Digital ISBN: 978-1-64080-746-4
Library of Congress Control Number: 2018934253
Trade Paperback published July 2018
v. 1.0

Printed in the United States of America
∞
This paper meets the requirements of
ANSI/NISO Z39.48-1992 (Permanence of Paper).

To Kate McMurray with my sincerest gratitude for her help.
And, as always, to my mom.

# CHAPTER 1

"CRAP. IT'S after seven." Danny Reynolds flicked a glance at the wall clock before switching off the last of the fluorescent lights inside the library. He could have kicked himself for losing track of time, but he always got caught up when putting together new exhibits for the library. He still hadn't settled on next month's theme, hence the little piles of paper and collections of Post-its all over his office. And maybe he also got a little distracted reading when he should have been working. Still, when you lived in an area trafficked by things that went bump in the night—and not all of them friendly, as evidenced by the latest rash of attacks—you needed to be more vigilant about the time. Most sane people made damn sure they were indoors before nightfall these days, and at this time of year, the nights were entirely too long.

Grabbing his coat, he rushed from his office, flipping up his collar as he prepared to face the colder than usual October temperatures. He rubbed at the knots in his stomach as he reached the door. *You'll be fine, Danny. Keep your eyes sharp and move fast.* He hesitated, leaving his hand resting on the cold metal for a long moment. Then he blew out a slow breath, clenched his keys in his fist prepared to gouge any would-be attacker, and pushed open the door that led to the employee parking lot. He stepped out into the windless night, the cold air nipping at his cheeks. Out of habit, he scanned the parking lot and street beyond. Empty. The library hadn't gotten around to replacing the single floodlight that illuminated the tiny gated lot yet, so he appreciated the meager light the crescent moon offered. *Better than walking home in the pitch-black.*

Danny shivered, and goose bumps rose on his neck. The cold seeped through his clothes even as the quiet stillness of the night unsettled him. He almost screamed when something thumped in the nearby dumpster. He stared at it, heart pounding for a long moment before yellow glowing eyes stared back at him. He pressed his hand to his stomach. Damn raccoon. He fought back the nervous laugh that wanted to escape. *I need to get the hell out of here and head home now before I make myself so paranoid I wind up doing something ridiculous, like spending the night locked in my office, curled up under my desk.* He turned to ensure the door had closed and locked behind him. He jerked on the handle once, then started to step away. A body slammed into him from behind, and stars exploded behind his eyes when his head smacked the door. Thin, wiry arms wrapped around him like bands, and his attacker pinned him to the wall. Adrenaline surged through Danny. His body all but buzzed with terrified energy. His breath rasped in and out as he jerked against his captor, struggling in earnest. He couldn't compete with the inhuman strength of the arm trapping him or wrench free of the hand clamped over his mouth, muffling his scream. Fear knotted his gut as a male voice growled in his ear.

"Didn't anyone ever teach you not to roam the streets alone at night?"

He suppressed a shudder as the fetid heat of his assailant's breath wafted over his skin.

"What's a pretty thing like you doing out after dark?" His attacker chuckled, a dark, ugly sound, as he pressed Danny even harder against the door. Danny struggled to breathe past the crushing pressure.

*Fuck, fuck, fuck.* Again, Danny tried to kick and fight, but damn, this thing was strong.

"Nothing to say?"

Pain shot through him when his assailant wrenched his head to the side, exposing his neck. He drew his tongue along the path of Danny's carotid artery. Danny gagged, his eyes watering from the pain of having his hair pulled. Trying to tug free sent lightning bolts of agony through his scalp.

"No matter, sometimes a nice quiet meal is just what one needs."

Just when he thought his heart would pound out of his chest, the creature struck. Sharp fangs pierced Danny's skin, penetrating deep. Waves of pain racked him. He went deaf to all but the blood roaring in his ear, breath hissing out of his nose. The vampire moaned in delight as though sampling the finest wine.

*I will not die this way. Not at the hands of some psycho vamp.*

That one thought resounded in Danny's mind as he redoubled his efforts, struggling as hard as he could, praying for even the smallest of opportunities to break free. The hand covering his mouth slipped lower, giving Danny the chance he needed. With no hesitation, he clamped his teeth on the exposed flesh, breaking the skin; the coppery taste of the vampire's blood flooded his mouth. A howl of pain and rage all but deafened him. The viselike grip of the vamp's arms loosened, but instead of hitting the pavement, Danny found himself airborne as his assailant flung him away. He slammed into the dumpster, both knees buckled, and he slid down into a pile of debris.

Gathering his strength, Danny scrambled to his feet. For the first time since the assault began, he saw his assailant's face. He was pale, even for a vampire, tall, and gaunt. His sick, skeletal appearance belied his strength. The deep red glow in the depths of his eyes, the wisps of foam about his mouth, and the snarl on his face made him look like a rabid animal.

*Please God, get me out of this alive.*

"Look, I don't want to fight you," Danny said, bracing for a second attack from his wild-eyed opponent, backing away while searching for anything he could use as a weapon. "I just want to go home."

The vampire's dark rumble of amusement sent an icy chill down Danny's spine. "Don't bank on doing either. You fight like a fucking girl, scratching and biting. You're pathetic." The vampire sneered. "I'm going to put you out of your misery."

*Oh shit, oh shit. Think, Danny, think.* He scanned for an escape route, or possibly the cavalry riding to his rescue, all the while keeping his eye on the creature who wanted to kill him for food and sport. There was no one in sight. Nowhere to run. *Where the hell are the Purity patrols when you need them?*

He glanced at the library door. He hadn't locked it, but there was no way he could outrun this thing. It moved too damn fast.

He saw the creature's shift out of the corner of his eye, the vampire's muscles bunching just before he sprang at Danny. He tried to scramble away, but the tackle caught him in the chest, taking Danny to the ground. The vampire knelt, placing his full weight on Danny's arms. Though he bucked and twisted, he couldn't budge the demented vamp.

"Now, where were we before you bit me like a fucking pansy? Oh yes, you seemed to want to get a taste of me. Why not have a little more?"

The creature slit his own wrist with one long nail. Then he gripped Danny's jaw, forcing his mouth open. He cackled as blood poured from his veins into Danny. Though he gagged, spit, and sputtered, Danny couldn't prevent some of the coppery liquid from sliding down his throat.

"Do you see why we love this? The flavors, the sensations, the power, it's a real rush," the vampire said, quirking a dark eyebrow at him and then leaning closer.

"Get off me, asshole," Danny gasped.

"Dirty talk makes me horny." The vamp laughed and ground his crotch against Danny.

Danny could feel his erection pressing against him and had to stifle a shudder.

The vampire licked at his still-oozing wrist. "Had enough?" He loomed over Danny, his hot, rank breath huffing in his face. Danny bucked and fought, even knowing the futility of his efforts.

"Doesn't matter, it's my turn, anyway." In a blink, the vampire shifted his weight and struck again, sinking his fangs into Danny's neck.

The change in position gave Danny the opportunity he needed. Bending his knees and tucking his feet close to his butt, he bridged up, unbalancing the vampire as he rolled, reversing their positions. Danny hissed at the pain of sharp fangs tearing through his flesh, but he kept moving, scrambling to his feet. Momentary excitement at a year's worth of jiujitsu lessons finally paying off flashed through him and then vanished when the vamp grabbed him from behind and flung him to the ground. He saw stars when he hit the blacktop, but he shook it off and tried to scuttle away.

Out of the corner of his eye, he saw a piece of a broken cargo pallet just out of reach. He lunged for it, grabbing it just as the vampire launched at Danny. Danny twisted back, armed and prepared to defend himself. Clasping the broken piece of wood, he held it out in front of him like a stake.

Danny saw the vampire's eyes flare wide with the knowledge that he couldn't stop his momentum. A wild scream rang out as the vampire impaled himself on the makeshift weapon. With a gasping gurgle and a stunned expression on his face, the life left the vampire's eyes as his limp form fell on Danny.

Danny lay under the heavy body, breathing hard for a moment before shoving it aside and pushing to his feet. He reached up and touched the torn flesh of his neck. Blood trickled through his fingers as he applied pressure to the wound.

He could only assume the creature was dead, but he didn't want to take any chances of having to go another round with him. Danny gave the body a final glance, grabbed his stuff, and raced the few blocks home.

DANNY SHOT up in bed, snatched from sleep by a burning pain radiating up his arm. He cradled his arm to his body, his hand throbbing in agony as though he'd been scalded. He flexed his hand to inspect it and blinked, unable to believe his eyes. A reddened, blistered strip of skin ran from the back of his hand almost to his elbow. *What the hell?*

He swung a leg over the side of the bed. He jerked back when pain like a red-hot needle being shoved in his calf shot through him. His chest tightened. Acid churned in his stomach. He stared at the thin strip of sunlight that snuck through a gap in his blinds and angled across the side of his bed.

Not possible. Danny slid a finger into the beam of light. Again, smoldering pain. Danny gritted his teeth and continued to hold his finger in the light. In seconds his skin began to smoke like paper under a magnifying glass, and the faintest scent of burned hair teased his nose. He snatched his hand back, jamming the finger in his mouth. *What the ever-loving fuck is happening to me?* His heart pounded and bile rose in his throat, leaving an acrid taste in his mouth.

He reached up to touch the bandage on his neck. Breath dammed in his lungs. "No." He rolled off the opposite side of the bed and rushed to the bathroom. He turned the tap on full blast and thrust his hand under it, letting the cool water ease the lingering ache.

He glanced in the mirror, and his pale, haggard reflection stared back at him. The gauze taped to his neck was not quite as stark as it had been last night. *My God, I'm a hot mess and all because I didn't pay attention to the stupid clock.* He pulled his arm from the water, dried it, and tossed the towel on the counter. His skin remained an irritated pink, but he'd otherwise healed. The angry blisters had disappeared. *Impossible.* He glanced back in the mirror and again eyed the bandage on his neck. He sucked in a deep breath, reached up, and peeled back the edge of the tape. He hesitated a moment before lifting away the entire covering. His mouth fell open, and his heart sped up.

"No freaking way." The flesh of his throat, while still angry and red, had almost completely healed. He struggled to pull in a full breath, and he braced himself against the vanity. "It's fine. I'm fine. The triple antibiotic worked super fast. That's all." *Yeah, right.* The memory of that damn vampire's blood slipping into his mouth and down his throat rushed through his mind so strong he could almost taste the coppery liquid.

He rushed from the bathroom to the kitchen mumbling to himself. "I need coffee or vodka, maybe both."

He headed straight for his coffeepot. The aroma of freshly brewed coffee filled the air and for some bizarre reason made him a touch queasy. *No. This cannot be happening. That fucking vamp did not turn me.* He balled his hands into fists, determined to do one damn normal thing today. He poured himself a cup and got halfway through when his french roast made a break for the exit. Danny lunged for the kitchen sink.

"Milk must have been bad." His stomach cramped. *No, it isn't. You know damn good and well what's happening to you.* Danny shook his head. Not possible. Not from just a little blood. It didn't work like that. At least he didn't think it did.

Still, he went back to the fridge, pulled out the carton, opened it, and sniffed. Not spoiled. With a shrug he took a testing sip straight from the carton and then gagged. He made a dash for the sink and spit out the swallow of milk as his throat revolted against accepting the liquid.

He coughed and sputtered, then sucked down a deep gulp of air. Bracing his hands on the edge of the sink, he locked out his elbows to keep his arms from shaking. He hung his head, squeezed his eyes shut, and continued to draw in long shuddering breaths.

"No. No, no, no. This can't be happening." Even as he fought to deny what he knew, his body trembled and his lungs fought to take a full breath. When darkness crept in around the edges of his vision, he slammed a fist down on the counter. He focused on the pain singing up his arm and used it to fend off a full-blown panic attack.

He whirled, determined to do something productive, but what? He couldn't go see his doctor or to the emergency room. Vampires were treated like monsters. Humans that got turned were treated like lepers. He could lose everything if word got out.

He glanced down at his hand and studied the pink, raw skin on the back. It looked better than it had fifteen minutes ago. He shook his head. Turning didn't happen like this, not as far as he knew. Turning took longer than this and took more blood than he'd ingested, but he could be wrong. He'd never really looked into it before.

Calm came over him. Research. This he knew how to do. He walked into his bedroom, made sure the blinds were shut, and pulled the curtains closed over them. He grabbed his laptop off his desk and climbed onto his bed. Settling in, he opened then booted the computer. He had access to the library databases and Google to help him. Hopefully he could find answers there, but if he couldn't....

He blew out a breath and dragged a hand through his hair. If research got him nowhere, well, he knew someone who might have some answers. That is if Kieran didn't boot him out the door on sight.

"YOU MUST consume the heart of the vampire who turned you? Yuck!" Danny shut his laptop and released a heavy sigh. He'd spent the better part of the day going through site after site, database after database, researching blood disorders, stomach disorders, and anything he could find on vampirism. The pickings on that last topic sucked. Few clear facts about vampires existed. Most of the data he found consisted of myths, lore, and wild speculations. After hours of digging, he knew little more than when he'd started.

He glanced up to find that the bright yellow tendrils of sunlight that kept trying to creep around his blinds had faded, muted. He looked up at his clock *5:30. Wow. Talk about disappearing down the rabbit hole.*

He rubbed at his dry, strained eyes and rolled his shoulders, attempting to relax tight, tensed muscles. His stomach grumbled and a gnawing ache settled in, equal parts hunger and worry. He could eat enough to bankrupt a buffet right about now, but he doubted he'd be able to keep it down.

Nothing in his research had even remotely mentioned anything that sounded like his current collection of symptoms. *What if there's no fix for this? What the hell am I gonna do?* He shook his head. He knew exactly what he had to do. It's what he'd wanted to do for a while now, but he'd been stalling. How do you walk back into someone's life after all but running screaming from them? No choice now. If he had fangs and red glowing eyes in his future, he needed all the information he could get, and he only knew one expert on the subject.

He shoved his feet into sneakers, rose, and then headed for the door. He dragged on his coat and grabbed his keys, but this time when he clasped the doorknob, his hand showed no evidence of injury. Even the faintest trace of redness had disappeared.

He closed his eyes, drew in a breath as he pulled open the door, and prayed that he wouldn't combust the second he set foot into even the tiniest bit of daylight. He eased his hand into the stream of sunlight. Nothing. He swayed with relief. *Finally, something is going right today.* He pulled the door open, stepped out into the fading light, and headed for his car and a very uncertain reception.

"LOSING YOUR touch, Kier?"

Laughter burst out from the small crowd surrounding the pool table when he botched a simple bank shot.

Kier chuckled good-naturedly. "I guess I'm just off my game tonight." He stepped back from the table and gave a rueful smile and a shrug as his opponent proceeded to sink his three remaining solid balls followed by the eight ball.

"Good game, man." He high-fived his friend. "The next round is on me." He collected the empty beer mugs littering the high tops around the pool table and headed for the bar. He slipped behind the counter, nodding at the regulars who waved and called his name in greeting.

"Alex, everything good?"

"It's fine. I've got this. Go away." His bartender and best friend all but shooed him away.

Kier laughed, poured a fresh round for his four companions, grabbed a bottle of water for himself, and then headed through the bar to the pool table.

"Okay, gents, who's up for another game?"

"I'm game." His challenger selected a cue from the rack. Kier rounded to the head of the table and leaned down to break. Just as he took his shot, a familiar and unexpected scent teased his senses, one he hadn't encountered in almost six months.

He scratched, causing a fresh round of ribbing to begin. Any other time Kier would have given as good as he got, the smack talk almost a bigger competition than the nightly games of pool. At the moment, though, any smartass comeback he could offer escaped him. Time stopped as a wave of heat, equal parts anger and desire, rolled through him. He breathed deep again. It couldn't be him, but there it was: that sweet, rich scent with just a hint of vanilla.

Kier straightened and handed off his cue with an absent thanks, then made his way to the door of the game room. At six at night, things weren't in full swing. In a few hours people would be crammed in, filling the bar with a writhing, rowdy sea of people. At the moment the crowd was thin. He did a slow scan of the throng. He took in the scattering of dancers on the small dance floor, scanned the faces of the people sitting in the booths and tables that ran the edge of the dance floor and down the length of the bar. He studied the reflection of the faces of the people who lined the bar. Then he honed in on the man standing in the entrance, the owner of that intoxicating scent. Danny Reynolds. He studied the tall, slim blond bundled in a gray pea coat. His cheeks flushed from the cold. Still as gorgeous as he remembered. Kier drew in a long breath and shored up the walls that locked away all the desire, frustration, longing, and hurt that wanted to race through him. *He must have a hell of a reason to come here.* He'd find out what Danny wanted, then get him the hell out of his bar. He'd let Daniel Reynolds kick him in the stomach once. He wouldn't let it happen again. He closed his eyes for a moment, pushing the memories of their time together back into the furthest reaches of his mind. It wasn't something he wanted to dwell upon, not now, not ever.

"Hey, Kier, you playing or not?"

"Sorry, guys. Fill in for me. I need to take care of something."

He crossed the bar, weaving his way through the tables, ignoring the calls from various patrons, and stopped behind Danny, who'd stepped up to the bar. As he approached he noticed something off, a subtle change in Danny's usual scent. Something unnatural. Something in his fundamental makeup had changed. Kier frowned and tried to ignore his growing concern.

"Danny?"

He whirled around. Wide, worried chocolate eyes met Kier's.

"Kier! It's, uh, it's good to see you."

The man before him wasn't the healthy golden man who'd walked... no, run away from him months earlier. This version of Danny was pale and exhausted. He fidgeted as he searched Kier's face. His eyes seemed a bit too bright, and there was an air of desperation that clung to him.

"What are you doing here?" Kier kept his tone flat, indifferent.

Danny laughed, the sound nervous and tight. "I was just in the neighborhood, thought I'd stop in."

Kier narrowed his eyes at Danny as he crossed his arms.

Danny shifted from foot to foot, and then he sighed and his shoulders sagged. "Kier, please. I need to talk to you. Privately."

"I'm pretty sure you said more than enough six months ago."

"I know. I know I was an ass, but this is important. Life and death important."

Kier stared at this man who'd once meant so much to him and debated. He didn't know if he was ready to hear anything Danny had to say. But he couldn't turn him away.

"Come with me." Kier turned and started through the crowd. Against his better judgment, Kier led Danny to an office at the rear of the bar. He walked to the mahogany desk that sat in the middle of the room, turned, and leaned against the edge.

He watched Danny as he took in the office. "It still looks the same."

"I'm happy with my space the way it is. Why would I change it?"

Danny nodded at the picture. "You kept it. We picked it out together, so I figured you might have taken it down."

Kier shrugged. "It's a nice piece." He crossed his arms.

"Yeah, it is." Danny offered a weak smile.

"Look Dan, I don't imagine this is easy for either of us, so why don't you tell me what you want. Why are you here?"

"Kier, I…." Danny shook his head. "Maybe this was a mistake, but I've got nowhere else to turn."

Kier leveled his gaze on Danny and watched the man's every move. Danny kept shifting his focus around the room with occasional glances at him. He couldn't keep his hands still. His entire body seemed to vibrate. Danny didn't tend to fidget, but this was the second time in the span of a few minutes that he caught him doing it. Danny appeared ill at ease, no longer at peace within his own skin. Kier wanted to pull him into his arms and soothe him, but they didn't have that type of a relationship anymore. Instead he gripped the edge of his desk and waited.

Danny paced, then turned to face him. Kier noticed that his hands trembled as he shoved them through his hair. He blew out a breath, then leveled a gaze on Kier that punched him in the gut. Kier read fear, pure and simple.

"I need help. I didn't know who else to turn to." He took a step closer, raised a hand to reach out, then dropped it. Instead, he rubbed his hands on his thighs. "Something's wrong with me."

"Wrong with you? What do you mean?" Kier frowned. "Are you sick? You kind of look like crap, by the way."

"Getting attacked will do that to a person." Danny shrugged as he hugged himself.

"Attacked?" Kier tried to maintain a level of detachment in his tone even as he snapped to his feet. He managed to halt his actions before he reached out to touch Danny and forced his hands into his pockets.

"Vampire. Last night." Danny opened his coat and tugged down his shirt collar. He ripped the bandage away from his neck. The punctures had healed, but the scars were still visible.

"Fuck, Danny. What the hell happened?"

Danny told him, in graphic detail.

*He could have been killed.* Kier dropped his chin to his chest and clenched the edge of his desk. Needing to breathe. To get the horrible images of Danny lying dead in the street out of his head.

"It's only been twenty-four hours and already a ton of strange things have happened to me. My other bruises and scrapes from the fight healed overnight except for these burn marks that I got from sunlight exposure, and… I can't seem to eat anything. I'm so damn hungry and scared, and if I can't figure out what is going on with me soon, I might just lose my mind." Danny's voice shook and his stomach growled. Unsteady, he moved over to the short beige couch and collapsed onto it. He covered his face with his hands. "What do I do, Kier? What's happening to me?"

Kier's gut clenched. He had no defense against the fear that emanated from his former lover. The plea in his voice battered at the wall around his heart. No matter how hard he tried, he couldn't be the cold-hearted bastard he'd planned on being if he ever encountered this man again. He clenched his teeth and his fists. Then he blew out the tension and moved to crouch in front of Danny. It might kill him, but he couldn't turn away the scared man huddled on his couch. He reached out, hesitated, then laid a hand on Danny's knee.

"What have you gotten yourself into?"

"I don't know," Danny snapped as he shoved his hands into his hair. "I was just going home, and I got jumped by psycho vampire from hell. It's not like I went out looking for this, you know."

"I'm sorry. That's not what I meant." No, Danny hadn't looked for this. Hell, he'd run from Kier and this world. What Danny needed right now was his help, not his condemnation.

"I need you to walk me through this. None of this vampire's actions make sense. With Purity getting more and more dangerous and fanatical in their actions, hunting on the streets has become a rarity."

"Hunting on the streets?" Danny's eyes went wide. "And you wonder why people fear vampires to the point of hatred. Humans tend to like their top-of-the-food-chain status."

"Hunting like that was never condoned."

"So, there is a form of hunting that's acceptable?"

"No. There are other, easier means to get the sustenance that we need."

"Like what?"

Surprised by the questions, Kier studied Danny. When he'd learned Kier was a vampire, not only did he refuse to hear him out and try to understand, he ran so fast in the other direction he all but left skid marks. Kier flashed him a raised eyebrow. "With Purity on patrol for vampires, it was just easier and safer to feed at one of the clubs or havens like this bar. Right now, though, we need to focus on you, not a rogue vampire. I have to say, I've never heard of such a small taste of vampire blood causing so many problems, though. It's like you're changing, but not completely. Like you're stuck in transition. Being a vampire is an all-or-nothing proposition. You either are or you aren't. There is no middle ground."

"Trust me to be something new and different. I always wanted to be a trendsetter, but not like this." Danny gave a weak laugh.

"Damn, when you get into trouble, you get in deep." Kier tried to sound lighthearted even though there was nothing lighthearted about the situation.

Danny's stomach growled again. He rubbed his abdomen, the look on his face pure misery.

"I've got an idea, but you probably won't like it. Just wait here." Kier left the office before Danny could ask questions. The less the man knew the better. He quarter-filled a mug from the special tap behind the bar, then returned to his office.

"Here, drink this." He handed it to Danny.

"Is this blood?" Danny stared in horror at the dark liquid in the mug.

"Don't ask, just drink." Hell, he'd crave it by the bucketload if he was transitioning; he might as well get used to the taste now.

"I can't drink this." He thrust the mug back at Kier.

"Look, you asked for my help. Don't argue with my solution. You may have no choice in this matter. Now drink, dammit."

Danny sighed, pinched the bridge of his nose, swallowed, then grimaced. "How do you drink that stuff?"

Kier shrugged. "It's an acquired taste. How do you feel?"

He watched Danny closely; if nothing else the blood had put a little color back into his face. Danny was going to hate knowing that something that repulsed him actually seemed to help him. Then in a flash Danny's expression changed.

"Oh God." Danny groaned as he clutched his belly.

Kier had him in the bathroom in an instant. When the sickness passed, Kier closed the toilet lid and helped Danny sit. After wetting a cloth, he handed it to the exhausted man, who was now paler than when he started.

Danny wiped his mouth, then pressed the towel to the back of his neck. When he looked up, Kier saw tears pooling in his eyes. *Ah, damn.* This was not how he'd planned his night. He'd never expected to see Danny again, had finally moved on. Now here he was, fucked by fate. Kier laid a hand on Danny's shoulder. "We'll figure this out, Danny."

"I don't know how much more I can stand of this. Is there a plan B?"

"Plan B is taking you to a doctor."

"I seriously doubt my doctor is going to know how to fix me." Danny hunched into himself.

Taking Danny by the elbow, he helped him to his feet. "The one I have in mind just might."

# CHAPTER 2

*Twenty-Three Hours Ago*

"COMMANDER ROGAN, I think you should take a look at this?" The voice crackled over the radio.

Michael Rogan glanced over at the walkie that lay in the passenger seat of his Jeep and sighed. He knew that voice too well. It belonged to a rookie member of his squad, one whom he heard from a little too often. Sure, he meant well, but he called in for the littlest and sometimes stupidest reasons. Still, given a bit more experience, he'd be far less jumpy and a darn good soldier. However, on a night like tonight, when all Rogan wanted to do was finish his patrol and return to headquarters, he wished the kid would adjust faster.

He reached for his radio as he continued to cruise past the darkened storefronts that lined the mostly empty streets. Despite being the home to a sizable college, Sinclair still rolled up the sidewalks by nine o'clock. The growing fear over the recent vampire attacks had shoppers and store owners getting home as early as possible as the days got shorter and dark sooner. Generally, he was a live-and-let-live kind of guy, but the sooner Purity could get them under control, the better. People should feel safe in their own neighborhoods, day or night.

He pressed the button on his walkie. "What is it, soldier?"

"We've got a body, here?"

Rogan gritted his teeth. *Dammit.* This body made the seventh in as many weeks. "You know the drill. This isn't the first time we've come across a vampire kill." It likely wouldn't be the last, either.

"This is different, sir. This is a dead vamp. I really think you need to see this."

Rogan frowned. A dead vamp was a dead vamp, but something in the rookie's voice concerned him. "What's your location?"

"Employee lot of the public library, sir."

"I'll be right there."

Tossing aside the radio, Rogan make a U-turn in the middle of the empty street and accelerated the Jeep.

Five minutes later, Rogan drove into the library parking lot. He parked just outside of a taped-off area illuminated by a portable floodlight. Climbing out of the Jeep, he called out to his men. "What have we got here? Have you called the cops yet?"

He approached the cordoned-off area, noting the sprawled body of a thin man, a large piece of wood sticking up out of his chest. He glanced at his men, noticing the pallor of their faces, the distressed furrow of their brows as they watched him approach. He crossed to the scene, ducked under the tape, and walked to the two fatigue-clad men. All eyes shifted to the body. Rogan noticed a familiar pair of scuffed red combat boots. He closed his eyes, pressed his fingers to them for a long moment. When he looked again, he shifted his gaze to the lifeless face. *Shit!*

"Okay, no cops. This one stays in-house, understood?"

The men nodded.

"Have you called for a cleanup team?" He snapped out the demand.

"No, sir, we wanted you to see this first before we contacted anyone."

Rogan nodded and grabbed the radio off his belt.

"Headquarters, this is Rogan, come in."

"This is headquarters, go."

"I need cleanup at the employee lot of the Sinclair Public Library. Now."

"Acknowledged. Team is being dispatched. ETA is fifteen minutes."

Rogan hooked the radio back on his belt.

"That's Jared Lydecker, isn't it, sir?"

Rogan glanced up at the young soldier, who couldn't be more than twenty-three. His wide eyes locked on the body at his feet as he swallowed hard. "Yeah, it is. You two are going to make sure this site stays pristine until the team gets here. Radio squads 3 and 4 to get over here and have them start an area search. If anyone even thinks they saw something that can help us figure out what happened here, I want to know about it. Understood? I have to go in with the body and report to Lydecker."

"Yes, sir."

He turned, irritation and relief swirling in his gut. He'd joined Purity years ago when it was a fledgling private organization just starting to gain traction. Fresh out of the Army, getting into security made the most sense to him. Purity offered him a heck of a lot of money to basically do what he'd been doing before. He helped to keep the community safe and trained new soldiers. Unlike being on the police force or in the military, the odds of him getting shot at were slim to none. With a family to care for, the offer appealed greatly. Instead, he wound up spending his days cleaning up after Lydecker's son, Jared. Jared should have been eliminated ages ago; he should have been put down like the rabid beast he'd become. Rogan couldn't be sorry someone had done the deed for him, but he did not want to deal with the coming shitstorm.

A heap of what looked like old rags and insulation moved, and a low moan emitted from it. All three soldiers whirled, guns at the ready. Rogan approached with caution, ready to fight if necessary. He leaned down, gripped a dirty blanket, and yanked it back. Dark bloodshot eyes glared up at him from a grubby face.

"What the hell, man? I'm sleeping here."

Rogan jerked the homeless man to his feet, then whipped his head away as the pungent aroma of unwashed body and an excess of alcohol accosted his nose. "How long have you been here?"

"How the hell should I know. I don't have no damn watch. Got here a bit after dark. Found a soft spot to sit and, uh, relax a bit, then fell asleep."

"Did you see an altercation that happened here earlier?"

The man frowned, swaying a bit when Rogan released him. "Didn't see a fight. Heard a fight, but didn't see it."

Rogan glared at the man. "You hear someone being attacked and you did nothing?"

The man just shrugged. "What was I gonna do?"

Rogan opened his mouth, closed it, then shook his head.

"Looks like the one guy made it out okay. Lucky break finding that piece of wood."

"I thought you didn't see anything."

"Said I didn't see the fight, and I didn't. But I needed to pee. When the shouting stopped, I climbed out of blankets and saw him lying there and another man running away."

"So, you pissed, then went back to sleep."

The man shrugged again. "He was dead, the other man was gone. Ran off that way." He pointed down the sidewalk that wrapped around to the front of the library.

"You climbed back in your pile and went back to sleep? You didn't think to contact the authorities."

"Warm in there. Didn't want to lose my spot. 'Sides, he's gone. Nobody can help him now."

*Truer words.*

Rogan looked at the two soldiers. "Stay here. Make sure the scene isn't disturbed. When backup gets here, fan out. I want some men here on the site. The rest should search around the library and see if they can find anything to help us figure out exactly what happened here. We need to track down the other man involved. We could have a huge problem on our hands." *Especially if he ingested any of Jared's blood.*

"WHAT PART of I don't want to be disturbed did you not understand? If you want to keep your job as my assistant, you need to learn that *do not disturb* means just that."

At the sound of the barked dismissal, Rogan rolled his eyes and pushed open the door to Dr. Thomas Lydecker's lab.

He crossed to the gray-haired scientist who sat at a table on the far side of a state-of-the-art laboratory scribbling notes in his journal. He stood waiting for Dr. Lydecker to acknowledge him, but he continued to scribble in his notebook. Rogan gritted his teeth. "Dr. Lydecker, we need to talk."

Lydecker shot up a single finger, finished his note, then glared up at Rogan. "What do you want? Why are you here disturbing me?

You know I don't like being bothered when I'm working. I am this close to having a working formula for my genetic reversal serum. I can feel it. In fact, I might have had it already if you people would leave me alone."

Rogan crossed his arms. "Are you done?"

Lydecker narrowed his eyes at Rogan. "Who do you think you're talking to?"

Rogan wanted to say a pain-in-the-ass mad scientist but checked the impulse. Now wasn't the time. Instead, he raised an eyebrow at the man.

Lydecker leaned back in his chair and huffed out a breath. "What is it?"

Rogan pushed his black beret off his head, stepped into the laboratory, and stood tall, almost at attention. "Sir, I'm sorry to report that we found your son while we were out on patrol near the public library."

"What do you mean found? That's not possible," Lydecker scoffed. "Jared is sedated and secured in one of the containment rooms. He got a little overexcited."

Rogan shoved his hands in his pockets and drew in a long breath. He might not like the man much, but no parent should ever get a death notice on their child. "I'm sorry, sir, but Jared is dead."

Lydecker blinked and shook his head.

"Not possible. He's still in his rooms."

"No, sir, he's not. Somehow he managed to escape."

Lydecker's mouth opened, but no sound emerged. He shook his head again. "No. I locked Jared's door myself." He shoved off his stool and away from the lab table, heading for the door. Rogan followed him. Together, they rushed down the shadow-filled hallway. Lydecker muttered denials with every step. When he reached the first of the containment rooms, he slid open the small viewing window and peered into the secured room beyond.

"Jared?"

No answer. Lydecker hammered his fist against the door. "Jared. Answer me." He grabbed the ring that attached to a retractable cord on his belt and fumbled for the correct key. He unlocked the door and then rushed in, calling for his son. Rogan followed him, not wanting to leave the distraught man alone. He trailed Lydecker from kitchen to sitting area to bedroom. All empty. When they entered the small bathroom off the bedroom, they found dust, debris, and a bent vent cover lying on the floor. Lydecker clenched his fists as he stared up into the large, dark, open hole of the ventilation shaft.

"No!" He shook his head and looked back at Rogan. "No, dammit." In that moment, all the energy seemed to drain from the man. He took one last scan of the empty cell and then braced his hand on the wall. "You're sure it's him?" His voice broke on the last word as his entire body sagged.

Rogan cleared his throat so he could answer. He had his differences with the annoying scientist, but his gut clenched at the sight of this father in pain. "I'm sure, sir."

Lydecker turned and headed for his laboratory. He moved as though lead filled his shoes. "Where is he?"

"His body is on its way in. I'll let you know when he arrives."

Lydecker nodded and continued down the hallway until he reached the door to his lab. He pulled it open and then trudged in. With shoulders sagging, he dropped into a chair. His head dropped back, and he stared up at the ceiling.

"I just needed a little more time. I was so close to having a new serum, and this time it would have worked. It would have cured him of his horrible affliction. I could have changed him back into the bright, ambitious young man he'd been before they made him a monster."

"I'm sorry for your loss, sir." Rogan reached out and patted his shoulder.

Two soldiers pushed a gurney holding a black body bag into the laboratory.

Lydecker approached the table, fists clenched at his sides. He stared down at the black bag, his entire body tensed. He pressed his lips together, and then reached for the zipper tab. He clasped it between two fingers, the metal to jangling from his trembling. Then he whipped his hand away as though the zipper became white-hot.

"Who did this?"

"We don't know, sir. When we arrived, we found your son, signs of a fight, and some blood."

"I want a full investigation. Do you understand? Find the person who did this to Jared and bring him to me."

"Yes, sir."

"Good. Now get out. I've got work to do." He dismissed all of them with a sharp wave of his hand.

The two soldiers filed out of the room. Rogan turned to do the same.

"Rogan."

He looked back at Lydecker, who stared down at the bag again. "I want whoever did this alive."


"MIKE."

"Dammit. Does she have me microchipped?" Rogan muttered to himself as he turned and watched Melissa Moran, the number two person in charge of Purity, stride toward him. He didn't know how she always found him in the five-story building with its twisting maze of hallways. But she always popped up out of nowhere like a ghoul in a haunted house.

"Melissa, do me a favor and get some hard-soled shoes."

"Why would I do that?" She smirked at him, but her cold ice-blue eyes remained expressionless.

"I was apprised of the Jared situation."

"Yeah. I feel for Lydecker."

She snorted. "It's sort of ironic and galling. All the money, time, and effort we've dumped into Lydecker's cure for his son and what happens? Jared breaks out and gets staked. Wasteful." She shook her head.

Rogan studied Melissa, not sure if she referred to the resources used or Jared's death. Odds were she meant both, but you could never really tell.

"Do we know what happened?" she asked.

"Basically, Jared got loose and attacked someone. I've got men going over the scene as we speak."

"Keep me in the loop. In fact, it might better to funnel everything through me. All Dr. Lydecker will care about are results, not the details. When your team finishes collecting evidence, let me know. I want our best people on the analysis."

"I can do that." He narrowed his eyes and gave her a slow once-over as warning bells chimed like mad in his head. She betrayed nothing of her intentions. Melissa Moran made an art of keeping her thoughts and feelings locked behind a wall of professionalism and suspect concern.

"Excellent. The faster we can get this situation resolved, the better. We need to get this organization back on track."

"What do you mean?"

She waved off the question. "Do we know anything about the other person involved?"

"No, whoever it was had gone by the time we found the body. There was a lot of blood at the scene. I'm not sure of exactly what went down, but we need to track down the victim."

"My thoughts exactly. We need to ensure that there weren't any repercussions from the attack. If there were, we should— address the issue."

"If this person was infected by Jared, perhaps Lydecker can help him. It would be good PR for Purity."

Melissa flexed her jaw. "The last thing we need is Lydecker finding a fresh test subject. I'm sure this latest development will only ratchet up his obsession with this damn cure." She sighed and pressed her fingers to her forehead.

"It could kill it. The whole point was to cure Jared. Now he's gone."

"Unlikely. That man is convinced a cure for vampirism is the answer. That it will end the tension and fear. Stop the attacks. It won't. It may treat the symptoms of the disease, but it doesn't change what these people, and I use that term loosely, have done."

"Come on. That's like saying finding a cure for cancer is a bad thing. Both are terrible diseases. If we could cure them, it would help a lot of people."

"Apples and oranges, Mike. Cancer patients don't opt in. Vampires do. Then they become monsters...." Her hands balled into fists.

Rogan cocked an eyebrow at her rare display. "Not all of them. What about attack victims?"

"They would have been better off dying."

Her words were so soft Rogan almost didn't hear her response.

Melissa rolled her shoulders and smoothed her hands over her hips. "I need to get back to work. Keep me in the loop. We need to get this resolved as soon as possible." She strode off without making a sound.

*She's up to something.* He didn't know what, but he planned to keep his eyes open.

# CHAPTER 3

*Present Day*

DANNY HUDDLED deeper in his coat, trying to escape the biting cold as he and Kier approached a three-story, redbrick office building that looked dated but well maintained. The small parking lot stood empty, as did the quiet suburban street it sat on. They made their way up a shrub-lined pathway to the darkened front door emblazoned with Total Family Care in bold blue letters. A white roller shade covered the windowed section of the door. Danny took a quick gaze up and down the street. No traffic, one lone streetlight, no signs of life from any of the surrounding houses.

"Kier, I'm pretty sure this place is closed for the day."

"Sharon is here. She's always here."

"Workaholic?"

"Yes, and she also lives here."

"I suppose that's one way to avoid a commute. But seriously, Kier, I have a doctor. What's happening to me is probably a bit beyond what conventional medical science can treat."

Kier huffed out a breath. It condensed into a cloud in the chill of the evening. "Do you want help or not?"

"Yes."

"Then shut it. If anyone can help, Sharon can." He pressed a buzzer. A minute later a female voice came over the tinny intercom. Kier stated his name in response to the inquiry. After a brief pause, the locks clicked open, admitting them into the building. They stepped into a waiting room filled with cloth-cushioned seats, battered magazines, drug advertisements, and a large aquarium alive with multicolored fish.

"It's a regular doctor's office. One, not what I was expecting. Two, have I mentioned I don't like doctors?"

"It *is* a regular doctor's office. Where did you think I was taking you?"

"Frankenstein's lab or at the very least, a specialist."

Kier rolled his eyes. "Sharon Stiles is the best shot we have at figuring out how to fix what's wrong with you." He crossed to the receptionist's window and yelled, "Sharon."

"Coming. Keep your shirt on."

Danny hadn't known what to expect of a doctor who treated vampires, but when the little sprite of a woman emerged from the door that led to the exam rooms, Danny's eyebrows shot up. She wore a lab coat over jeans and a tattered Harvard Medicine sweatshirt. She'd tied her dark hair back in a high ponytail, and cat-eye glasses sat perched on her pert little nose. All she needed was a backpack and an armload of notebooks, and the college co-ed look would be complete.

"Expecting Igor?" She winked at Kier.

"No! I, uh… just someone a little older, less cute." He covered his face with his hand. "God. Sorry, Dr. Stiles."

Sharon laughed. "I like him, Kier."

Kier grunted.

She laughed again. "Come on back." She waved for them to follow her through the doorway and showed them into an office loaded down with file cabinets, medical texts, and journals. She rounded the desk and claimed her seat in a large wingback chair that dwarfed her and made Danny think of an old Lily Tomlin skit. When she rested her arms on the desk and linked her fingers, her demeanor changed, and she became all professional. "Okay, boys, what seems to be the problem?"

"Sharon, this is Danny Reynolds."

Sharon's eyes went wide as she shot Kier a look. Then she schooled her face and focused back on Danny.

"Why don't you tell her."

Danny sat silent for a long moment. "Well, I…." He stopped, swallowed the lump that clogged his throat at the memory of the attack. He'd come so damn close to dying.

"Danny?"

"Well, last night I was attacked by a crazed vampire and now something is wrong with me. Oh, and doctors make me nervous." Danny's voice wavered a little at the end.

"I'm sorry to hear you were hurt, but if I'm going to help, I need a little more detail. I promise you I won't bite." She smiled and winked at him, flashing a fang.

A shaky laugh tumbled out of Danny. "Sorry. Remembering the attack isn't easy."

Kier's hand fisted, then released in his lap. He reached out, hesitated, then patted Danny's shoulder.

Danny took a breath, rubbed his hands over his thighs, and started from the beginning. He watched Sharon as he told his story. As he spoke, the gleam in Sharon's eyes got brighter and brighter. A long silence fell over the room when he finished.

"I'm so sorry you went through that, Danny, but this is fascinating." He could all but see the gears turning in her brain.

Kier frowned. "Sharon, he's not one of your science experiments. We just want to know if you can help him."

"I don't know yet. This is new to me too. I've never heard of anything like this happening before. I'm going to have to run a few tests and see what's what. But the obvious answer to the problem would seem to be turning him."

"Yeah, I kind of figured you were going to say that." Kier sighed.

"What! No!" Danny shoved up from the chair. His heart pounded. Blood roared past his ears, almost deafening him. "I don't want— I can't be a— There has to be another option?"

Sharon rose and rounded the desk. She took both of Danny's hands in her cool, delicate clasp. "Let's do tests, and then we'll see. We won't rush into anything. I don't know what's going on inside you. We're going to be smart and calm. And get to the bottom of this, all right?"

Danny shifted his gaze to Kier, then back to Sharon. So much whirled around inside him. Exhaustion dragged at him. He wanted to sit and breathe and have the world be normal for five minutes. He searched Kier's eyes for some understanding, some feeling, but cold blue stared back at him.

"Look, guys, let's go to my lab. We'll start with simple blood tests and take it from there. Sound fair?"

Kier shrugged. "It's your call, Dan."

Danny just nodded.

"Great! Come on downstairs with me. You might as well be comfortable while we do this."

"Have I mentioned that I hate needles?" Danny followed Sharon and Kier out of the office.

"Don't worry. Kier can distract you."

*Yeah, he sure could.* Once Kier had had distracting him down to an art form. Danny pushed the thought aside. *Neither the time nor place.* Besides, now he'd probably take more pleasure in jabbing him with the needle than diverting his attention.

Sharon led them down the hall to the rear of the office. She coded into a room that looked like an average medical supply room. On the far wall, there appeared to be a locked storage cabinet. Again, Sharon typed a code into the cabinet, and it opened to reveal a spiral staircase leading to a lower level. One by one they filed in, winding their way downstairs. Last one through the door, Danny stopped to shut it behind him. He tugged the door and grunted at the unexpected weight. He gave it another yank, and the door glided closed with a solid thunk and a loud click of locks.

"Sorry about that. It's heavier than it looks." Sharon glanced up and smiled. "Rule number one in the world of vampires is spare no expense when protecting your personal space."

"Good to know. Should I be taking notes?"

Sharon laughed. Kier remained stoic.

The lights from below illuminated their way as they descended. The stairs led down to a huge open space that flowed uninterrupted from family room to formal dining room to kitchen. Warm bronze and tans decorated the entire space, but each section had its own unique splashes of color.

"Wow," Danny murmured.

"Thanks, we like it." Sharon led Danny to the dining area and offered him a seat. Kier stood behind him. "I'll be right back." She left the room and disappeared down a hallway.

Kier laid his hand on Danny's shoulder. The solid weight of that contact sent a wave of warmth through him. Despite what lay between them from the past, he let himself take comfort from Kier's touch, his strong, reassuring presence.

When Sharon returned, she had a needle and tourniquet with her. She tightened the elastic band around Danny's arm, then kept talking as though she weren't about to stab a sharp metal object into his vein. "This building used to be a warehouse. My husband, Robert, and I converted it into not only our offices, but our home as well. Makes life easier when there's no commute between work and home." She smiled. "See that over there?" She gestured with her head.

Danny looked but saw nothing. "What am I looking at?"

"Nothing." When he looked back, she'd already slipped in the needle and was about to connect the first collection tube.

"I promised to distract you before I stuck you. Just keeping my word." A sly smile tugged at her lips.

"That was easy."

"Vampire. I'm good at taking blood." She winked at him. For the first time in twenty-four hours, all the pent-up tension and worry released. Her light, easy smile chased it away. It might have only been momentary, but he'd take it for now. "Why don't you join Kier over in the living room and make yourself comfortable. This could take a while." She gathered her tubes and started back toward the hallway she'd disappeared down earlier. Danny watched her depart into the darkness, then looked over at Kier. *Okay, Danny, you can do this....*

KIER CROSSED to the family room, dropped onto one of the plush red couches, and grabbed the remote. Switching on the television, he then flipped through the channels, stopping every so often to see if the show held any appeal. He left it on a channel playing some random crime drama. Out of the corner of his eye he watched Danny pace while tugging at his plump lower lip with his teeth. A low wave of heat rolled through Kier as he remembered sucking on and nipping at that lip. He could almost taste the clean, rich flavor of Danny's skin. Then it had all gone to hell. Kier shoved away those thoughts and tossed a mental bucket of ice on the heat that wanted to wind its way through him whenever he got close to Danny. Anything personal between them had ended six months ago. That had been Danny's choice, and he'd respect it no matter how much it still hurt.

"Sit down, will you? All the pacing is distracting."

"Sorry." Danny dropped into a chair opposite Kier. He leaned forward, bracing his elbows on his knees, shoved his hands in his hair, and breathed.

Kier balled his hand in his lap. He could smell Danny's worry. It took everything in him to resist going to Danny and holding him, to tell him that everything would be fine. Before he could stop himself, he lifted a hand, started to reach out, but wounded pride regained control. He redirected so that he rubbed at the back of his neck. Why couldn't he move past these feelings? Why couldn't he let go of the hurt? It shouldn't matter to him anymore, and it didn't. At least that's what he worked to convince himself. Still, he wasn't a complete ass.

"You all right?"

"Not even a little." Danny wiped his hands down his face and looked at Kier. "I-I'm sorry, Kier." Danny lifted his gaze to meet Kier's. Fear and a hint of regret shone in Danny's deep chocolate eyes.

"For what? Getting attacked? Having no one else to turn to but me?" Kier cocked his head. "Or maybe because there's a decent chance you're going to wind up becoming just like me? The very thing you ran screaming from." Kier shut his mouth with a click of teeth. He breathed in one, twice, reining in the angry hurt that wanted to lash out. *Not the time or place.* He shrugged and returned his attention to flipping through channels.

"Kier, dammit...." Danny leaned forward, reaching out a hand but stopping short of touching Kier.

"What?"

"Please."

Kier closed his eyes. Danny's plea chipped at his resolve. He looked back at that fretful expression. "What do you want me to do, to say? Do you want me to pat your hand and assure you everything will be fine? I could do that, but it'd be a fucking lie. I hope, for your sake, that Sharon has a solution to this problem that doesn't involve turning you. I really do."

"A lie would be welcome right now. I'm scared, Kier. My life is whirling out of control."

"This is just the beginning."

"Gee, thanks," Danny said. "You're real frigging reassuring." He slouched back in his chair.

"I know you don't want anything to do with this life. You made that abundantly clear when you all but ran out the door when you found out what I am. Forgive me if I'm not inclined to blow sunshine at you, nor am I going to sit here and pretend all is well between us."

"Kier, look, when we broke up. I reacted badly, there's no arguing that, and I've been wanting to apologize."

Kier glanced back at Danny. He saw the regret, heard the apology, but he couldn't allow himself to trust it.

"Look, don't worry about it. If nothing else, I know your true feelings, I know where we stand, and I've moved on." He gritted his teeth and reinforced the walls he'd built to keep what he felt for Danny tucked safely away.

"You don't know what I feel. You couldn't possibly." Danny shoved up from the chair, crossed to a shelf full of books, and started pulling off various volumes. He carried them to the dining room table, sat, and started scanning through them. Kier watch him struggle to decipher the texts. He flipped through one book, slammed it shut, and cracked open a second. "This is ridiculous," he murmured to himself before calling out. "Dan, what do you think you're doing?"

"Just a little research?" Danny puffed out his cheeks and shoved a hand through his hair.

Kier pushed up and crossed to him. He picked up one of the books and read the title. Danny had collected numerous volumes on blood disorders, genetic mutations, and gene therapy.

"You know the solution to your problem isn't in these books, right? If it were, Sharon would already have a fix for your problem because I'm pretty sure these books make a lot more sense to her than they do to you or me. Instead she's back in her lab muttering to herself and getting eyestrain peering through a microscope."

Danny's shoulders sagged. "I know. You're right, but I can't just sit around waiting on Sharon. If nothing else, this will keep me sane while I wait to learn if I'm going to slowly lose control of my body because some crazy vampire thought I looked like a midnight snack. First my brother, now me. At least he's still alive and fully human."

"Danny, there is good and bad in every group. You've had the misfortune to see more of the bad side of vampires, but don't paint us all with the same brush."

"What else should I think of someone who tried to kill me?" Danny crossed his arms over his chest.

Kier mirrored his stance. "I'd call him severely disturbed. I'd call him an aberration. I'd call him something you're not going to find any information on in these books."

Danny worried the corner of one of the glossy book pages between his fingers. The texture of the smooth, cool paper against his skin seemed to help settle him. Danny looked up and met Kier's gaze.

"Did you know that I spent the last few months reading everything I could about vampires?"

Kier snorted. "Typical Danny. Instead of talking to me, learning from me, you ran back to your precious library and buried your head in dusty old tomes that are filled with more fiction than fact when it comes to vampires."

Danny slammed the heavy textbook shut and shoved to his feet, stepping up to Kier.

"Okay, educate me. What makes a vampire a vampire? What medical miracle created this alternative race of beings?"

"Beings, well, I guess that's a step up, but maybe just try referring to us as people. That's what we are. We're not the monsters that Purity would like you to believe. If they have things their way, they'll convince the public that we should be eradicated."

"Dammit, Kier, can't we get past this? I already admitted that I reacted poorly, but you don't get to keep playing the injured party here. You're just as at fault as I am. You lied to me. Granted it was a lie of omission, but a lie is a lie."

"Just like you had your reasons, I had mine."

Kier dropped into a chair and rubbed the back of his neck. "Not much is known about how or where vampires originated. Even less is known about how conversion works. It's only recently, since vampires made themselves known to the world, that studies have begun to understand the process. Sharon is one of the scientists researching the topic."

Danny leaned toward Kier, gripping the sides of his chair. "You've been around since time began. Someone must know something, anything that can help us." Danny closed his eyes and bowed his head.

Kier laid his hand on Danny's arm. "I promise you Sharon is working as fast as she can."

Danny looked up into Kier's eyes again, lifted his hand to cover Kier's. "Thanks for being here for me."

Sharon came wandering out of the hallway she'd disappeared down earlier, muttering to herself and scribbling in a notebook. She looked a little perplexed and a lot excited. Both Kier and Danny rose, waiting for the results of the tests like two innocent men waiting for the verdict of their trial. She continued to stand and scribble until Kier finally broke.

"Sharon?" Kier called her name louder than necessary, startling her from her thoughts.

"What? Oh sorry, boys. This is one of the most fascinating things I've ever seen."

"Doesn't answer the question, Shar. Is he transitioning or not?"

She pressed her lips together for a moment and looked upward as though searching for the right words. "Kind of. There's really not a simple answer to this." She turned and headed back toward her lab and waved at them. "Follow me. Let me show you." She led the two men into a long room that reminded Kier of a high school science lab with gray tile flooring, white resin lab tables with black tabletops, and walls of glass-fronted cabinets ringing the room. She stopped at a table that held three microscopes and a centrifuge. She looked through the eyepiece, adjusted the focus, then stepped back and gestured for Kier and Danny to look.

"There's an anomaly in Danny's blood. I've never seen anything quite like it. Normal vampire blood cells are smaller and darker than human blood cells. But yours are a strange hybrid of the two. Take a look." Danny bent to look at the three different slides Sharon had on display: human, vampire, and finally his. He didn't have to be a scientist to see some clear differences between the slides. It looked as though the vampire blood was slowly invading his human cells, but the final cell wasn't quite human or vampire.

"What exactly am I looking at, Sharon? I can see the difference, but I don't understand what's happening."

She perched on a lab stool and pushed up her glasses. "When a human is turned, the vampire blood infects the human cells, converting them to vampire cells. The process usually takes about twenty-four to forty-eight hours to complete. However, it usually takes a great deal more blood than you've told me you ingested to bring about the change."

"Shar, I appreciate the vampire biology lesson, but can you cut to the chase?" Kier crossed his arms and glared down at her.

"Patience, Kier, I'm getting there." She looked back at Danny. "Your attacker is quite the unique specimen. Something was wrong with him."

Danny snorted. "I'll say. He brought new meaning to crazy."

"True, but not what I mean. His blood was very potent, yet weak at the same time. Potent in that it took very little to bring about this partial change, but at the same time his cells couldn't complete the change. At this point, Danny is neither human nor vampire, so his body is freaking out. It's manifesting this *freak-out* through the list of symptoms you've already given me. I wouldn't be surprised if more changes occur as his cells continue to morph. I need time to study this further. His condition is an amazing find." Her violet eyes again gleamed behind her glasses. She swiveled on the stool and started jotting in her notebook again. Kier shook his head. She'd kicked into full-on scientist mode, and there'd be no stopping her now. Poor Danny would get poked and prodded more than a pincushion. Kier had spent enough time with her and her husband to recognize it in both of them.

"Danny isn't your lab rat, Sharon."

Danny gave a shaky smile. "It's okay, Kier. If she can help, I'm willing to be a test subject."

Kier nodded, but his stomach knotted. Danny becoming anyone's specimen didn't sit well with him. "So, what now?"

Sharon placed a gentle hand on Danny's shoulder. "I simply don't know. I need to bring Robert in on this, do more testing. In the meantime, you need to stay with Kier. You can't go home. You can't be alone. We really don't know what's coming next. I wish I had better news for you, Danny, but right now you're going to be stuck in a state of limbo for a while longer."

"What about food? I'm going to starve to death while you try and figure this." Danny's face went paste white, eyes wide and wild. A loud stomach growl filled the air. Again, Kier's gut clenched. This time in sympathy.

"We're not going to let that happen. In fact, I've got an idea. Come with me." They left the lab and followed Sharon to the kitchen. She pulled ingredients out of her refrigerator, set them on the counter, then got a blender and a glass.

Danny held up a finger, trying to catch her attention. "If it's anything like Kier's idea, been there, done that, threw it up already."

"Go sit in the dining room. I'll be in in a few minutes." She shooed them both out of the kitchen.

Kier and Danny crossed to the dining room, leaving Sharon rooting through her kitchen. They both claimed seats at the long red table. A few moments later, the banging started, followed by a few swear words. Then a blender motor sounded. Danny shot Kier a wide-eyed look.

"Is she okay in there?"

"The culinary arts were never her specialty." He wiped a hand across his mouth, covering a smile.

"Kier, a little help in here."

Kier raised an eyebrow but rose and went to the kitchen. Five minutes later, they returned. Sharon placed a glass on the table in front of Danny.

"A strawberry shake?" Danny gave the glass of pink frothy liquid, then Sharon and Kier, a dubious look.

She jammed her hands on her hips and narrowed her eyes at him. "Just drink it."

Danny lifted the glass, sniffed it, then sipped with caution and waited to see if his stomach would rebel. It complained a little but seemed to accept the drink. He took a few more sips. When the shake didn't make a mad dash for the exit, he smiled. "What did you do? What's in this?"

"A little of this, a little of that. Kier has the recipe. For now, you're going to be on a soft-food diet."

Danny rose and hugged the tiny vampire to him.

"We'll figure this out. Just give me a little time." She patted his back, then released him.

"Thank you. Thank you so much."

"Don't thank me yet. Now, why don't you go get some rest? You're going to have a lot to deal with over the next little while."

"Thanks, Sharon." Kier leaned down to hug her, then turned to Danny. "Come on. Let's get you settled."

"We, uh, could stay at my place if that would be easier."

"No, it's fine. I think we'll be better off at my house." Kier couldn't keep the resignation out of his voice. Great, nothing like an awkward situation with your ex to cap off your day.


DANNY AND Kier stepped into the foyer of Kier's townhouse. Soft light illuminated the small entryway. Danny paused, shrugging out of his coat and taking in his surroundings. He'd missed this place. It held a lot of good memories. He and Kier had spent a lot of time locked away here, just the two of them. They'd also imploded in a spectacular fashion here as well. He moved to hang his coat in the hall closet when he noticed Kier heading down the long hallway toward a door at the other end.

"Where are you going?" Danny hung back in the entrance, not sure if he should follow.

"To bed. It's been a long day." Kier slid a key into the lock on the door.

"Don't we need to go up for that?" Danny edged closer but only came about halfway down the hall.

"No."

Danny's stomach knotted even as he proceeded forward on leaden feet. "Something else you neglected to mention to me?"

"Don't start, Danny. Not now. I'm not up for that particular discussion right now."

"I don't recall you ever being up for that discussion."

"Look, just like Sharon, I protect my true home as well." Kier started down the stairs.

Danny stood frozen at the top of the stairs, his rioting emotions threatening to overwhelm him. As crazy as it seemed, something inside screamed at him that descending these steps meant walking away from his old life, maybe forever.

"You coming?" Kier called up to him.

"I...." Some of the panic and indecision must have shown in the expression on his face, because after a moment's hesitation, Kier climbed back up and held out his hand. Danny stared into Kier's brilliant ice-blue eyes. For one moment, the wariness in Kier's eyes dimmed and allowed a touch of the compassion that his stoicism had masked all night to shine through. In that instant, the man who Danny never managed to get out of his heart stood waiting for him. Danny grasped the offered hand and let himself be led down into a large, comfortable open space. Soft, cushiony sofas, a corner fireplace, and deep plush carpeting gave the room a warm, homey feel. A home that Kier had never shared with him.

"You've got a nice place here." Danny rubbed at the ache in his chest.

"Thanks." Kier gestured at a chair. "Make yourself comfortable. If you're thirsty, help yourself." He pointed to a bar that held a minifridge at the far end of the room. "I'm going to get your room ready. We'll get you settled in for tonight. Tomorrow, we can stop at your place and pick up some things that you'll need."

"Wait, what?"

"Dan, didn't you hear what Sharon said? You're probably going to be here a while. Figuring out how to help you isn't going to be a fast thing. What's happening to you is something new. Until we develop a game plan to manage it, you need to stick close. So you may as well be comfortable."

"Right. Sorry. My brain is a bit fried at the moment." Danny stood in the middle of the room, turning in a slow circle, taking everything in.

Kier slipped away, disappearing down a dark hallway that Danny assumed led to the bedrooms. He sank down into the sofa and dropped his head back so that he stared up at the ceiling. Exhaustion made his entire body heavy, and the adrenaline that had driven him all day leeched from his system. It left him in desperate need of sleep and turning his brain off for a few hours. How much more would get dumped on him? How much more could he handle? He shivered and rubbed his arms.

"Are you cold?"

Danny jumped and twisted to find Kier standing a few feet behind him.

"A little."

Kier snapped his fingers and the fire blazed to life. Danny's jaw dropped. He blinked at Kier once, twice, then goggled at the flames. "How did you do that?"

Kier smirked. "It's a gas fireplace. Sound activated. What, did you think I could light a fire with the snap of my fingers?"

Danny huffed out a shaky laugh.

Kier snapped his fingers again. This time a tiny flame danced above his fingertip.

Danny groped for the arm of a couch and then pushed to his feet. Gaze locked on the dancing flame, he moved toward Kier.

"Why did I not know you could do that?"

Kier shrugged and snuffed the flame. "It would have been a little difficult to explain being able to light fires at the snap of a finger without telling you the whole story."

"Why did you hide it from me?"

Kier gave him a "seriously" look.

"Don't give me that look. I freaked, I admit it, but you weren't exactly Mr. Honesty yourself."

"Danny, get real. I met you outside an antivampire book club. However, I didn't realize you were with them at the time."

Danny crossed his arms and glared at Kier. "It was a support group for victims of vampire attacks. It was a safe place for victims and families of victims to talk about their experiences and losses at the hands of those vile, vicious creatures." He all but spat out the words. When he met Kier's eyes, hard ice stared back at him. *Shit.* "Kier, I'm sorry. I wasn't thinking. I didn't mean—"

"Yes, you did. You meant every word of it, but keep in mind you're now staying with and being medically treated by two of those vile creatures."

"That's different. You're different." Danny reached a hand toward Kier as his chest went tight.

"Vampires, like humans, have the good and the bad among them. Maybe you need to think about that in the future."

"I know that. Kier, please." Danny stepped closer to Kier.

"Do you? Think about what you just said, and then consider why I kept my mouth shut about what I am. I just wanted you to get to know me first. I thought maybe…." Kier shook his head. "Doesn't matter now." Keir turned away and headed for the fridge behind the bar. He pulled out a bottle of water, twisted it open, and took a long drink.

"Yes, it does." Danny trailed after Kier and forced his words out through clenched teeth as anger, regret, and longing battled for dominance. "Maybe things would have been different if you'd just told me the truth from the start, but you let our relationship grow on a lie. If you'd only told me—"

"I did tell you and we already know what happened when you found out. You ran, and I didn't hear from you for six months. You probably wouldn't even be here now if it weren't for your predicament," Kier snapped.

"That's not true, but think about where I was coming from at the time." Danny gripped the edge of the bar, knuckles going white. His head started to throb.

"I know exactly where you were coming from—a place of fear and anger. Instead of thinking of the man you knew me to be, you burrowed back into your world of hatred and blame." He slammed the open bottle on the bar top, spewing a stream of water into the air. His scorching blue gaze burned into Danny's for endless moments. Then he sighed and dragged a hand down his face. All of the energy and emotion flowed from Kier like water down a tub drain. "This isn't the time for this discussion."

"Well, when is?" Danny leaned, wanting Kier to reengage. He hadn't intended to open this discussion tonight, but he didn't want to let it go. Not yet. Not with so much unresolved. Not when he could see Kier retreating behind the wall of indifference he'd built between them.

Kier rounded the bar and headed toward the hallway.

Danny threw up his hands and let them flop down at his sides. "So now what?"

Kier paused but didn't turn back. "Now we go to bed. We can't do anything more tonight, and arguing about the past isn't going to accomplish anything. After we wake up tomorrow, we'll figure out our next step. For now, I'm beat."

Danny dragged his feet but followed. Kier stopped at one of the guest bedrooms and waved him in. "Bathroom is across the hall." He skimmed his eyes over Danny's face. "I'd suggest skipping food and drink until breakfast. They may be a bit big, but I left a T-shirt and sweats for you to sleep in. Good night." With a nod, he started for his room.

Danny opened his mouth to speak, hesitated, then took the chance. "If you're still so angry with me, then why are you helping me?"

Kier turned in the entrance to his bedroom. Danny studied his former lover's eyes. Weariness, resignation, and irritation shone. "Because, like I already told you, I'm not an asshole. I'm not going to sit by and let you die because of what went down between us." Silence stretched between the two men. "Look, it's almost dawn. We both need rest. Just go to bed, Danny." With that Kier disappeared into his room, closing the door behind him.

Danny stepped into his room; the simple space held all the basics. He crossed to the bed and picked up the T-shirt Kier left for him to sleep in. He changed into it, not even caring that it hung on him like a dress. Then he crawled into bed, but sleep wouldn't come. His brain wouldn't shut off. Worries pinged around like ricocheting Super Balls. *How the hell did I get here? What the hell am I going to do if they can't fix me?*

Thoughts looped through his brain until his eyes and body grew heavy. Before he drifted off, one final thought slipped through his mind, a question that had nagged at him for the past few months. Could he and Kier possibly forgive each other and just maybe have a second chance?

# CHAPTER 4

ROGAN ENTERED Purity HQ at eight o'clock in the morning. He'd gotten home after midnight and woke up to find at least fifteen emails updating him on the status of the investigation into Jared's death and three voicemails, two from Lydecker, one from Melissa. It was going to be a long day. He made his way to the top floor of the building to Lydecker's lab. The harsh scent of bleach assailed his nose as he stepped into the large white room.

"Dammit!" Thomas Lydecker shoved up from his rolling stool, lab coat flapping, hands fisted in his hair. He tugged at it as he growled and then kicked his stool so that it flew across the room and slammed into the wall.

"Is there a problem, sir?" Rogan stuffed his hands into the pockets of his cargo pants and waited by the lab door. Let rant begin in three... two... one.

"I've been up all night analyzing some of the samples your team collected from the scene of—" Pain flashed in his eyes, and he swallowed hard before continuing. "Well, from the scene."

"Sir, you didn't have to do this yourself. We've got a team of scientists that we pay well to do all of this."

Lydecker snorted. "This is my son we're talking about. Do you seriously think I'd trust anyone else with this?"

Rogan pinched the bridge of his nose. "Sir—"

He waved away Rogan's concern. "Relax. You collected plenty of samples. There's enough left for our team to do a thorough secondary evaluation." He snatched a stack of papers off his desk and waved them in the air. "My son, my precious son, even in death gave me a gift."

Rogan cocked his head. "I'm not sure I follow."

Again, Lydecker shook the sheaf of papers. "He left me a way to continue my work. He found me a new subject for study."

"Okay. So what's the problem? I'm sort of lost here, sir."

"Do you see this?" He thrust out a hand toward the computer screen. "No match. How could there be no damn match in the system? I've been searching almost all night and nothing. We've got no record of this wondrous revelation. I can't continue my work until we find him. So, tell me you have something."

"We're working on multiple leads, sir. We hope to have something soon."

"Work faster." Lydecker threw down his papers, and they hit the table with a loud slap and scattered a collection of writing utensils, sending them clattering to the floor. "It shouldn't take this long to find one person. With all the cataloging and tracking Purity has done over the years, there must be some record of the creature with this fascinating blood profile. This amazing scientific find." His voice went dark and menacing, causing goose bumps to form on Rogan's arms. "This man took my son from me. The least he can do is help me complete my work."

Rogan cleared his throat, needing to ease some of the tension that had rushed in to fill the room. "We're doing the best we can, sir. Moving as fast as possible, following up every lead. We're going to interview the library staff, but they won't be in until ten. With luck, we'll get some information that will lead us to the victim."

"Victim?" If Lydecker could shoot lasers from his eyes, Rogan would have been sliced in two.

"Sorry, sir. Jared's assailant."

Lydecker smoothed his hand over the wild disarray of his salt-and-pepper hair, but he only made matters worse. From his expression, Rogan couldn't tell if the man wanted to explode again or not. He remained quiet, waiting while the doctor made a visible effort to settle. He straightened his lab coat, adjusted the collar on his shirt, and then sucked in a breath.

"Rogan, I know I've asked before, but it's more important than ever that I stay up to date on the progress of your investigation. This person is vital to my research. In fact, I think he can help take it to the next level."

Rogan just nodded. The doctor might be an overzealous old man, but he was also a grieving father. Rogan actually felt sort of bad for Lydecker. "Can I ask, sir, what makes this individual so special?"

Lydecker's face lit up like he'd just won the Nobel Prize. He reclaimed his rolling stool and scooted over to the microscope, peered through the eyepiece, adjusted a few nobs, then glanced up. He waved his hand, gesturing Rogan over. "Come here, look."

Rogan crossed to the table and leaned down to view the slide.

"Do you see the miraculous little blood cells on the slide?"

"Yeah, I think so." Rogan stood and eyed the doctor, noting the excited gleam in his eyes.

"Those cells are almost identical to Jared's, but the DNA analysis shows that this blood isn't Jared's." Lydecker grinned at him like a kid getting his first science kit.

"This all sounds fascinating, sir, but I have to admit science was never my strongest subject."

Lydecker sat, energy seeming to drain out of him. Rogan had a flash of guilt that his comment seemed to take the wind out of the doctor's sails.

"I am so close. So close." Lydecker fisted his hand and pounded it against his thigh.

"That's terrific, sir."

"I've put in countless hours to create a serum to reverse the effects of the vampire's curse. Jared, my poor, weak-willed child." Lydecker's voice broke. He cleared his throat, then continued. "He inspired all of my research, and the drug I'm creating works, almost. It's designed to prevent the body from producing vampire cells and to begin reproducing normal human blood cells, but it wasn't quite strong enough. Jared's cells, like those of his unknown assailant's, were hybridized, a combination of both human and vampire."

Rogan frowned. "Am I looking for a vampire, then?"

Lydecker shook his head. "No. The number of hybrid cells in this sample is small. I'm pretty sure what we're looking at is the beginning of a conversion. But since it's with Jared's weakened vampire blood, this individual may or may not be able to fully convert. I'm not sure. This is all new. But I do believe he will reach a point where his blood profile is extremely similar to my son's. Once we have him, I'll be able to complete my research. With a little more time and study, I'll find the cure. Although it will be too late for my poor boy, thousands will flock to us for help, and finally the world will be rid of this horrid affliction that rips families apart."

Rogan pressed his lips together and studied Lydecker; his stomach turned like he'd eaten something that didn't agree with him. He held no great feeling for vampires one way or the other, and having a cure for those who wanted it could only be a good thing. Right? They wouldn't really try to force it on all vampires, would they?

"Your serum would be just for those who want to be human again?"

"Perhaps, at first."

Rogan's gaze met Lydecker's. Something flickered in the scientist's eyes, something dark and unsettling. Rogan took a step back. Again, his stomach churned. Purity's job was to keep vampires in check and, in his opinion, to keep humans from taking the law into their own hands. But to force conversion, that didn't sit well with him. It didn't sit well with him at all.

"I should let you get back to it, then." Rogan headed for the door, hands balled into fists.

Lydecker smiled and nodded. "Yes, there is much to do. Finishing the cure will be a fitting memorial to my son, and we'll get there. But not until we find this specimen. He's the key that will unlock the formula." He leaned down to look into the microscope, then reached for his notebook to jot down more notes. "Maybe we should consider putting together a task force just to focus on the search for this person. I don't understand how he's not in our database. Not in any database. We need to expand our cataloging. I want this individual found. Collect him, but do it without making a scene. We don't want him trying to run during acquisition and some *concerned citizen* interfering."

Rogan's jaw went slack. The hand that had been about to press the door latch fell limp at his side. "You want me to kidnap this man? But, sir."

"That's such an ugly term. I prefer to think of it as involuntarily acquiring his time and services."

Rogan couldn't look at him. He couldn't keep the shock and disgust off his face. He hadn't always agreed with the orders he'd gotten from Melissa and Lydecker—he'd somehow managed to rationalize all of that away—but this....

He pushed through the door into the hall, ready to hand in his resignation for the first time in the five years he'd worked for them. His cell phone beeped. He snatched it from the holster on his waistband. This better not be goddamn Melissa. He sighed and settled a bit when he saw the picture on his phone screen. His brother Brian stared up at him with a big goofy grin on his face, shining brown eyes, and Mickey Mouse ears on his head. He'd taken that shot on their trip to Disney to celebrate Brian's high school graduation two years ago. He smiled when he swiped to read the message.

*Hey Mike. Tuition bill came today. Ouch. PS—I stole some cash from your sock drawer. ;-)*

That one short message threw a bucket of cold water on the remainder of his fury. What the hell was he going to do? College tuition money wouldn't just land in his lap, but he'd make sure his baby brother got the best education he could afford. As much as he wanted to, he couldn't just quit, and finding another job in the next eight hours—so not happening.

He jammed his finger into the Down elevator button. He needed out of here right now. Rogan growled when his cell phone rang as he shoved out the front door that led to Purity's parking lot. His growl changed to a groan when he checked the screen to find Melissa's name displayed.

"What?"

"Have you found the person who killed Jared yet?"

The cool, unamused tone grated on him. "We're interviewing the employees at the library this morning. Hopefully that will help point us in the right direction."

"Under no circumstances does Lydecker get that information before me. You got it?" She snapped out the words. That she'd let the calm professional mask slip even this much surprised Kier.

"I take it you heard about Lydecker's results."

"Yes. Unbelievable. I'd hoped this little mission of his would have died with his son. What are the odds, Rogan, that he'd find a replacement?" Her breath came hard and fast through the phone.

"I have no idea. But if you want me to track this guy before anyone else, you need to let me go so I can do my job. If one of my men locates the subject first, I can't and I won't order him to lie to the doctor. You're not the only person we report to."

He could swear a low growl came across the phone line. "Just find him."

"I will." He disconnected the call. "But I make no promises that I'll turn him over to either one of you."

Rogan frowned. Melissa's lack of support for Lydecker's work was one of the worst-kept secrets at Purity, but this level of anger seemed unwarranted. He didn't like it. He didn't like being stuck between crazy and crazier. Being given orders that contradicted each other and for that matter given orders that were flat-out illegal. His gut told him he needed to watch his back, especially around Melissa. He huffed out a breath and climbed into his Jeep. First, he'd find this man, and the rest he'd figure out from there.

MELISSA MORAN slammed the door of her lab. The metal door hitting the frame made a satisfying boom that echoed off the concrete walls. She marched to one of the long black resin-topped lab tables and pounded her fist into it. "No. No, no, no. This is not possible. Millions of dollars wasted on his pointless experiments, and just when it looks like it's over, he finds a viable replacement. Un-fucking-believable." She pounded the table one last time, then braced, taking measured breaths, trying to regain her composure.

When her body stopped shaking, she smoothed her hands over her hair, then her shirt before she adjusted her skirt. She crossed to her computer and switched it on. While it booted she took one of the blood samples she'd taken from Lydecker's lab over to a microscope, prepared a slide, and then slid it on the stage. She peered through the eyepiece. Sure enough, the cells had the same appearance as Jared's.

"This is unacceptable. I will not let this continue. We will not continue to throw good money after bad attempting to cure these disgusting creatures. Make them human again? Let them pollute the human race with their tainted blood? I don't think so. No telling what freakish mutations will occur if these 'formerly' infected *people* are allowed to mix and reproduce with normal humans."

She started various test runs on the other samples she'd procured. The machines in her lab hummed as they worked. Satisfied with her progress, Melissa turned from her table and faced the cage at the far end of the room. She stopped at a small white refrigerator and pulled out a full bag of blood before crossing the room toward the lone figure that lay curled on a cot inside the cage with his back to her.

Stepping up to the cage, she slid open a metal door and shoved the bag through so that it hit the floor with a plop.

"Dinnertime, Aiden," she said, sliding the door back in place. "Eat up. You've got to keep your strength up."

The figure didn't move, didn't respond.

"Aiden, don't be such a baby. You remember what happened last time you went on a hunger strike, don't you?"

"Go to hell," Aiden growled as he shifted on the cot and pushed himself to a sitting position.

Melissa suppressed the urge to shudder. Disgusting creature.

"Why don't you just kill me?" Aiden swayed a little, then leaned forward and snatched the bag off the floor.

"Because I've got plans for you."

"You say that every time I ask."

"And yet you persist in asking." She crossed back over to her instruments and continued to study, to take notes. She did enjoy her little chats with Aiden. He'd been here almost a month, and so far he was shaping up to be the perfect specimen for her little pet project.

"So what's the plan for today? Torture? More tests?"

"Today, I've got other things on my plate, so you get a little break, which I think you need. That last test seemed to be a little tough on you."

Aiden snorted and lay back on his cot. "No, not at all. Your intestines twisting themselves into knots is a walk in the park."

Melissa glanced up. Aiden held the blood bag, eyeing it with both need and wariness.

"It's safe to drink. I didn't do anything to it." She moved to her computer and started inputting data.

"And we both know how reliable your word is."

Melissa sighed. "I don't have time for your attitude. Drink it. Don't think I don't care. At some point you'll have no choice."

"Screw you." He spat out the words.

She narrowed her eyes at him. "Not in this life or any other. I wouldn't lower myself to allow your kind to lick my boots."

"I can't imagine anyone, man or woman, wanting to lick any part of you." The vampire sneered at her.

Rage exploded through her, sending heat through every cell of her body. "You know nothing about me." She ground out the words. "Vile creatures like you took everything from me. You shouldn't be allowed to walk amongst decent human beings. You're a blight on this planet, and you should be exterminated."

"Boyfriend leave because you're a fanatical bitch?"

"Two of your kind attacked my husband. Forced him to drink. You turned a wonderful man into an abomination. I had no choice but to kill him. To put him out of his misery. You and your ilk forced me to kill the love of my life." Pressure built behind Melissa's eyes as she railed at the vampire. Tears threatened to fall, but she refused them. She'd never let this beast see her cry. Never let them see the hole they'd made in her. She took a moment to collect herself. When she looked at him again, her shields were back in place. When she spoke she used calm, measured words.

"Your kind took something important from me. Now you're going to help me take everything from your species." She shook back her long hair. "Don't let your dinner get cold." She turned away and headed for the door. "I'm going to leave my project cooking for a while, but I'll be back soon. You may want to tidy up in there. You're going to have company soon."


ROGAN PUSHED through the revolving door of the Sinclair Public Library. At ten o'clock on a Monday morning, the only people in the building were the staff and a collection of senior citizens who appeared to be there for the retirement money management class advertised on one of the bulletin boards. He did a quick scan of the room, spotted the information desk, and zeroed in on a pretty blonde scanning and stacking books. Ramping up the power on his smile, he strode forward and leaned on the desk.

"Excuse me, ma'am. I'm hoping you can help me."

She returned his smile. Her eyes gave him a slow sweep. "What can I do for you, sir?"

"I'm sure you heard about the incident that happened here on Friday night?"

Her eyes went wide, and her hand fluttered to her throat. "I did! It's so scary. I can't believe that a vampire attack happened right in our parking lot. I know everyone who works here tries to be super conscious of the time, but sometimes it gets away from you. I think this will be a reminder to all of us here to be even more vigilant."

Rogan nodded. "That's a good plan, ma'am. Also, be sure no one leaves alone."

"Definitely, definitely." She picked up a pile of books off the counter, placed them on a cart, and then returned to Rogan.

"As I said, I'm looking into what happened. We're trying to figure out who the other person in the altercation might be. We want to check on the victim of the attack, make sure he or she is okay, and get them any medical attention that they might need. We also need to get a statement for the record."

She furrowed her brows and nodded. "Of course, that makes perfect sense."

"I'm wondering. Have all of the library's employees reported to work this morning?"

She bit her lip. "I think so. At least everyone full-time or part-time mornings."

*Damn.* Rogan shoved his hand through his hair. He'd been banking on the victim being a library employee. Tracking this person down would be next to impossible now. But then, that might be a good thing. No victim meant he wouldn't be a party to forced abduction.

"Oh, wait!" She laid her hand on his arm. "I don't recall seeing Danny Reynolds at all this morning. I can check with my supervisor to see if he called in, or maybe he's here and I've just missed him." She beamed at him like a little girl presenting a picture to her dad.

Rogan returned the smiled. "That would be greatly appreciated."

Her cheeks flushed pink. "Wait here. I'll be right back." She hurried off, her long blonde ponytail swinging behind her.

A few minutes later she returned, the bright smile she wore gone. Instead she worried her lip with her teeth. "I just spoke to the branch manager, and she told me that Danny hasn't reported in today. That's not like him at all. If there is one person you can count on to be on time, it's him."

"Perhaps I can go check on him. Would you be able to give me his address?"

She furrowed her brow. "Oh, I-I don't know about that. I understand you're investigating, but I just wouldn't feel right handing out his personal information without his permission or a warrant or something official like that."

Rogan resisted the urge to clench his jaw. He plastered a pleasant smile on his face and laid a reassuring hand on her shoulder. "I tell you what. I'll leave you my card. If Mr. Reynolds calls in or comes in, please pass it along to him and ask him to contact me. Or if you get the okay from him to pass on his info, please give me a call." He pulled a business card from one of the pockets on his cargo pants and handed it over.

A look of relief spread over her face. "Absolutely." She glanced down at the card, then back at him. "Michael."

"Just call me Rogan, and thank you again." He turned and headed for the door. His cell started playing Heart's "Barracuda" as he stepped out into the crisp morning air. Melissa. He needed to have his body checked for implants. No one had timing as good as hers. He tugged his phone out of his pocket and swiped across the screen to answer.

"What have you got for me?"

He hesitated for a moment as he contemplated lying. No, it would be better to find Daniel. He could control the situation better if he knew the locations of all players. Plus, he couldn't afford to get caught in a lie. Not now. "We're looking for a Daniel Reynolds. He's an employee of the library. He didn't show up or call in this morning."

"So, where is he?"

"I don't know."

An annoyed rumble sounded through the phone. Rogan furrowed his brow. The ice queen clung to her cold emotionless mask like a shield. So to see it slip more than once over the last day or so meant something.

"What do you mean you don't know?"

"I managed to charm the name out of one of the library employees, but she balked at giving me an address."

"Well, at least you got a name. Give me a few minutes and I'll see what I can dig up. Just sit tight." She disconnected the call.

Rogan rolled his eyes. "Good morning to you too." He headed for his car and the warmth of its heater. The car had just warmed up when his phone rang again.

"I've got a Daniel R. Reynolds at one twenty-four Park Avenue, Apartment B. I'm sending you a photo of him. Find him."

"And when I do?"

"Don't play dumb, Rogan. It's not a good look for you. You know what you need to do."

Again, Rogan frowned. "Fine. I'm on my way now." He hung up, put the car in gear, and pulled away from the curb. A queasy sensation rolled around in his gut. He didn't like this, not at all. Protecting people from a legitimate threat, fine, but he didn't sign on to be anyone's henchman. But he would go check on Reynolds because if Jared had hurt or infected him, it was his job to find out. For now, that's what he'd do: his actual job.

He drove the short distance to the apartment complex. He parked and then approached the front door of the building.

He counted himself lucky when he stepped into a small foyer only to find the inner door already propped open.

He climbed the stairs to the second level and stopped in front of Daniel Reynolds's door. He knocked twice and then waited. No response. He tested the knob and his luck held, because the door swung open.

"Hello?" He slipped into the apartment and found himself in a wide area that made up the living and dining rooms. He stood listening to silence. Again, he called out and again, silence. Not at work, not at home. Where the hell had this guy gone? People don't just disappear. He wandered into the bedroom. The covers lay rumpled on the bed, but otherwise Reynolds kept his space neat and organized. He checked the closet. Clothes hung in an ordered row. Nothing screamed, "I packed up and left town in a hurry." He moved to the desk, searched through the drawers, flipped open the laptop, and powered it up.

While he waited for it to boot, he rummaged through the bathroom and hit pay dirt when he noticed bloody bandages in the trash can and dirty, bloodied clothes in a hamper. He bagged them. If nothing else it would give Melissa and Lydecker something to keep them busy until he could track this guy down. Next, he did a quick check through a guest room, the kitchen where the below-sink cabinet stood open with the contents stacked on the floor, and a small laundry room. Nada. No papers or receipts lay out that could potentially give him clues to where Reynolds might have gone.

He headed back into the bedroom and sat at the small desk that held the laptop and a collection of framed photos. Most looked like family photos, but one had a different feel to it. It featured Daniel Reynolds and another man who stood with their arms around each other, smiling into the camera. He picked up that picture and removed the frame, hoping it had been dated and labeled. Lucky for Rogan, Reynolds's organizational tendencies extended to his photos as well. *"Kier and me." Okay, who's Kier?* Add him to the list of Reynolds's friends and family that Rogan needed to look into, but this one looked special. Just something about the way they were smiling together led Rogan to think they were more than friends. Using the camera on his phone, he snapped a picture. Then he called Melissa.

The moment the call connected, he began speaking. "Melissa, he's not here."

"Dammit." She hissed out the words.

"I've got a few leads I can follow to try and locate him. In the meantime, I think we need to have someone sit on the apartment. Reynolds has to come home eventually."

"All of these resources at our fingertips and we can't find one man. What is he, invisible? Do what you need to do."

"I've got samples from his apartment. I'll wait here until the surveillance is in place, and then I'll drop these off to you." Rogan exited the apartment, passing two maintenance men as he descended the stairs.

"Move your ass, Rogan. I don't have all day." Just before she disconnected the call, he heard her mutter, "Going to have to handle this myself."

Rogan just shook his head. Daniel Reynolds better hope Rogan found him first. Something told him that nothing good could come of Melissa getting her hands on him.

# CHAPTER 5

KIERAN WOKE just before sunset, as usual. He didn't need to see the afternoon sun fade to the blues and purples of twilight; his internal clock kept perfect time. Instead of rising and getting his day started, he lay in bed, his mind working. Just when he'd come to terms, sort of, with Danny's departure from his life, he reappeared. Not because he missed Kier and wanted him back, but because he was scared and had nowhere else to turn. Good old Kier, he'll help, he'll make it all better. He covered his face with his hands and blew out a breath. God, his life, one complication after another. Let's face it—all the anger in the world didn't stop him from having hot sweaty dreams about Danny. *I am so screwed.*

He threw back the covers and climbed out of bed. Slipping out of his bedroom without making a sound, he crossed the hall to Danny's room and eased the door open. Danny slept on. Dark circles took up residence under his eyes. His skin a sickly pale, he lay sprawled on the bed. He'd kicked away the covers, and the oversized T-shirt Kier had given him bunched around his midsection, revealing a strip of smooth, flat stomach. Kier tamped down the urge to cross to him and touch. To slide his fingers over soft warm skin. *Stop, dammit.* Kier clenched his fists, then backed out of the room, easing the door closed. He whirled and stalked to the bathroom. He yanked open the door of the large glass shower enclosure, wrenched on the water, and stepped into the crisscrossing sprays of multiple showerheads. He needed the water hot to clear his head.

"Get it together, McCade. Just buck the hell up and do what you need to do. You've mentored fledglings before. This is no different," he grumbled as he ducked his head under the water. "Don't fool yourself into thinking he came back for you. He doesn't want anything to do with you or your kind. He just wants to be cured so he can go about his life." He scrubbed a handful of shampoo into his hair. A smart man would foist Danny off on Sharon. She'd have a field day studying him. But he couldn't do that to Danny or Sharon. Danny needed him. A heavy weight settled in his chest as he envisioned all the time he'd have to spend alone with Danny. He couldn't pat him on the head and send him on his merry way. Danny couldn't go about life as he knew it, not until they got to the bottom of whatever was going on inside him. In the meantime, he needed someone to help him, monitor his health, and walk him through the rough patches, which were no doubt on their way.

"You can do this, Kieran McCade." He jerked on the faucet knobs, cutting off the water. He climbed out of the shower and went to get dressed for the night. Then he headed for the kitchen, where he found Danny sitting at the counter, head resting on his arms.

"Hey. You okay? You look like hell."

Danny grunted in response. It seemed to take all of his strength for Danny to raise his head and focus tired eyes on Kier.

"I'm hungry, tired, and grouchy. Just shoot me now." Danny moaned.

"The first two can be solved by feeding you and putting you back to bed for a while. The last creates more mess than it's worth. Newly turned vampires are a lot like newborns. They eat and sleep a lot."

Fear flashed through Danny's eyes, then disappeared. "I'm not a vampire."

"No, but you're not exactly human anymore either."

Danny hunched in on himself, and the growl of his stomach disrupted the silence.

"The 'just turned' hunger can be fierce."

"But I'm not—"

"You tell yourself whatever you need to get through."

Danny buried his head in his arms again and uttered a muffled "I'm sorry."

"For what?" Kier poured a cup of coffee, then went to the fridge and added a splash of blood.

"I'm being a big baby about this."

Kier took a long sip. "No, you're just being honest. You don't like vampires. You don't want to be a vampire. I get it."

"No. That's not it at all. I mean it is, but it's not. I don't hate vampires. Not all of them. But you can't blame me for being reticent after what happened to my older brother."

"What exactly did happen? You never told me."

"Kevin was out at a club one night with friends. It was getting late, and he had a final the next day. He was always super focused on his studies. Had great grades through high school and managed to make being geeky cool. So, one night toward the end of finals week, his roommates decide they're done studying—they either know it or they don't at this point—and they wanted to blow off some steam. They head out to a local club, but after a few hours Kevin decided to head back to his dorm. He wanted to be well rested for the exam. God, he was such a dork." Danny smiled at that and rolled his eyes. "Anyway, the rest of his friends decided to stay and party a bit longer. Kevin, the idiot, decided to walk instead of calling a cab or a damn Lyft."

Danny paused and stared at the counter. A red flush spread up his neck as his jaw clenched, as anger flared through his body. "A pair of vampires grabbed him off the streets, and for two days they beat him, fed from him, terrorized him, and raped him before he finally managed to escape." Danny paused, sucked in a breath. When he spoke his voice came out rough, strained. "He was never the same after that. Who could be? My brilliant, Tolkien-loving brother died that night."

Kier set his cup down. He couldn't breathe past the lump in his throat and the pain in his chest. He inhaled long and slow. Blew it out. When he looked at Danny again, he hadn't moved. His gaze remained fixed on the counter. The muscles in his jaw, arms, and hands clenched and unclenched.

Kier crossed to him and laid his hand over his fist. "I-I don't know what to say, Dan. I'm sorry. I'm so sorry that happened to him. I'm sorry about everything your family had to endure as a result of the attack."

Danny shook his head and gripped Kier's fingers. "It's not your fault, but thank you."

"Is he doing okay now?"

"Living with the trauma of the attack has been hard on everyone. It was devastating watching Kevin struggle with the nightmares and the anxiety. We tried to get him help, but at first, he refused. He didn't want to talk to anyone about what happened. Slowly he started doing everything he could to hide away. At first, he avoided leaving the house alone. Then it progressed to not leaving at all. The PTSD got so bad he wasn't safe at home. He became a danger to himself and to Mom and Dad. The breaking point was when I got home one day and found him with a razor blade in hand." Danny paused, swallowed. "I found him curled on the bathroom floor, blood running down his arms."

"Please tell me he didn't kill himself." Kier dropped his chin to his chest, his dark hair falling over his forehead.

"No, he only made a few superficial cuts, but I think if he'd been left alone for much longer, he would have slit his wrist. I'll never forget the look of terrified hopelessness in his eyes." He took a long, slow breath. "I talked him into dropping the razor. Then I bundled him into my car and took him to the ER. We got him admitted inpatient and started getting him the help he needed. He attempted suicide once more. Thank God he never succeeded. He's been in and out of inpatient facilities. Now, he's a million times better. He still has some bad moments, occasional nightmares, but he's managed to get his degree, got a job, and he's starting to contemplate trying to live on his own. It's taken six years to get him to this point." Danny looked up, his eyes meeting Kier's.

"Did they ever catch the vampires who did this to him?"

"They did, and I think that's one of the things that helped him the most. Kevin wasn't their first victim. They'd done this to three other people before they were caught. Purity found them and stopped them. It helped Kevin to know that they could never get to him and hurt him again. One of his doctors gave information about the support group. The group really helped and, as luck would have it, led me to you."

"I'm glad it helped you. I really am, and I'm glad the vampires were caught." Kier wanted to take Danny in his arms and just hold him. Offer him strength and love. Just as he reached the brink of giving in to the urge, Danny's stomach grumbled again.

KIER SMILED and released Danny's hand. He crossed to the refrigerator, pulled out a packet of a deep-red liquid and a shaker bottle.

"Are you making Sharon's special shake?" Danny eyed the bottle, then looked back at Kier. Kier didn't answer; instead he cracked open a bottle of a high-protein nutrition shake and poured it into the shaker.

Danny shoved off the stool.

"Stop." Danny froze. "Sit." It never occurred to him to protest, so he hopped right back up onto his seat. A moment later he frowned, not sure what had just happened.

Kier continued to work. "What exactly are you adding to that? Is it what I think it is?"

Kier glanced over his shoulder and rolled his eyes. "I can either walk you through the recipe and you can do this yourself, or you can shut it and let me finish so that we can both eat."

"So, what you're saying is I'm better off not knowing."

"What I'm saying is sometimes you talk too much."

When he'd completed the drink, Kier grabbed a large mug, set it in front of Danny, and poured a thick liquid that looked like strawberry milk into it.

Danny stared at the mug. His mouth went dry even as his stomach growled again. "There's blood in that, isn't there?" He wiped a hand over his mouth as bile burned its way to the top of his throat.

"You have two choices. Drink it or starve. As I recall, starving wasn't your preference. Hurry up either way. You need to get dressed so we can head over to your place."

Even knowing he had no other choice, he still couldn't make himself readily accept that he needed to drink blood to survive. Vampires drank blood, not humans. *But you aren't exactly human anymore, are you, Danny?* He gripped the mug with clammy hands, sniffed. It even smelled a little like a strawberry shake, with a faint hint of metal.

"All right, Danny, you've got this." He suppressed a gag, held his nose, and chugged like a frat boy at a kegger. "Oh God." He gasped out the words and hung his head as he set down the mug.

Kier raised an eyebrow at him. "Nasty? I followed Sharon's instructions explicitly."

"No. It actually tasted good, and I'm trying to come to terms with the fact that I enjoyed that. Give me a second here." Danny went quiet and took a moment to assess. The gnawing ache in his gut disappeared, and energy infused him.

He looked up at Kier, who leaned against the kitchen counter, ankles crossed as he sipped from his cup of coffee. Nothing about flannel should be attractive, but the black-and-gray button-down with two buttons open at the collar with the low-rise jeans and bare feet had heat pooling low inside Danny.

He swallowed hard and rubbed at the back of his neck as he gave Kier a slow once-over. Despite everything, Kier could still make Danny's brain go fuzzy. With six feet of solid muscle, tousled brown hair, and blue eyes that could never quite mask his irritation, Kier made him want to forget everything and lose himself in Kier's kiss. Danny licked his lips.

Kier's lips twitched as though he fought back a smile.

"Dan, finish your drink. I don't have the time to stand here all day for your viewing enjoyment." Kier turned to rinse out his cup.

"Are you sure? Because that sounds like a fun way to pass the day."

This time Kier gave in and smiled.

"Tell me something. How old are you? Something you said made me think that you only look like you're in your thirties."

"I was born in Philadelphia in 1875. My parents immigrated to America about five years before I was born. My father worked on the railroads."

Danny blinked. "So that makes you what, almost one hundred and fifty years old. Wow, dude, you are seriously robbing the cradle with me."

Kier choked on his coffee. "Shut up, annoying child, and go get dressed. We've got things to do," he said, dabbing at the few drops of liquid that had sprayed on his shirt.

"But wait, I want you to tell me about the old days. What was it like to be alive to see the telephone invented? Did you ever wear a zoot suit? If so, are there pictures?"

"You're an ass. Have you always been this annoying?"

"Probably." Danny flashed a bright smile at Kier.

"What happened to the scared human who was revolted by all things vampire?"

"I told you, a lot of things about me changed in the time we were apart; I've been reconsidering a lot of my beliefs. I'm slowly coming to terms with everything. Don't get me wrong, I'm still terrified of everything that's happening to me and I'm still not sure that being a vampire is something I want for myself, but I've got you to help me through it. That means a lot to me."

Kier looked away from him, and any trace of humor disappeared. "Yeah, well. We-we have a lot to do tonight. We've got to stop by your place, pick up some of your stuff, and bring it back here. We're going to be spending a lot of time together for the foreseeable future. You'll want your own stuff."

Like the flip of a switch, Kier went from open to closed, hidden back behind some metal shield he'd erected. For the life of him, Danny couldn't figure out what he'd said to cause Kier's defenses to reengage. Some of the pleasure of the shared moment dimmed for Danny. He ran back through the conversation in his head, and with it came the memory of other conversations they'd had, things he'd thought and said. Kier was right. He was an ass. It never once occurred to him how Kier would feel hearing him refer to vampires as vile creatures, for justifying his break-up with Kier because of the lies. He'd never given Kier one reason to think he'd be receptive to learning the truth. He knew deep down even as he and Kier had their final fight that Kier didn't fit the stereotype of vampires he'd built in his mind, but at the time he couldn't move past it.

His heart squeezed. He couldn't blame Kier for his caution. He'd hurt him. Hell, they'd hurt each other, but if he could convince Kier that he really wanted to start over, maybe they could repair some of the damage.

Kier walked past Danny, heading toward his room. "Kier?" He blew out a breath and then pushed himself up and out of the chair.

"Yeah?" Kier stopped and looked back over his shoulder.

"Thank you for everything you're doing."

"You're welcome, Danny. Now stop thanking me."

Danny watched the long line of Kier's back and the roll of his hips as he walked away. Everything about the man was sexy. He huffed out a laugh. Who'd have thought he'd owe that crazy fucking vampire a debt of gratitude. He had no problem being stuck with Kier for a while. Maybe, just maybe, he could convince Kier to give him a second chance.

THE SILENCE abounded during the short ride to Danny's apartment. By the time Kier pulled into a spot in the parking lot behind his apartment building, Danny all but vibrated with tension.

"I've been thinking—"

Danny jerked at the sound of Kier's voice.

Kier raised an eyebrow. "You okay?"

"Yeah. I'm just stressed. Nervous, I guess."

"About what?"

Danny barked out a laugh. "Seriously? Sorry. When things get quiet, I get lost in my head thinking about everything. I mean, I'm about to move in with you. I just wish that the reasoning behind it was different."

"Right. I...." Kier flicked a glance at him and then shook his head and fell back into silence.

"What?"

"I've been thinking. You'll need to request leave from your job while we're figuring your situation out."

"Oh God. I haven't thought about work. I didn't even call in today. I'll email Brenda tonight. That's all I need is to lose my job."

"That may still happen."

Danny frowned at Kier. "Thanks for pointing that out, Captain Pessimism."

"I'm just trying to be real. We don't know how long this is going to take, but I don't expect that Sharon's going to have the answers overnight." Kier pulled his car into a spot at the rear entrance to

Danny's building and cut the ignition. "Come on. Let's go in and grab your stuff."

Kier climbed out of the car and headed for the building entrance, leaving Danny to scramble behind.

Danny coded them in. They made their way up the back stairs and then into Danny's apartment. "We can get Sharon to give you whatever type of paperwork you'll need for your job." Danny remained silent as he and Kier entered, shutting the door behind them. "No matter how this gets resolved, you're going to need some time to recuperate."

"You're probably right." Danny took calming breaths. He got overwhelmed every time they discussed the next steps in this process. He could handle the moments, but the bigger picture weighed a bit heavy and kept knocking him off balance. He headed for his bedroom.

"Kier, can you do me a favor and throw away any of the perishables? We can toss the bag in the dumpster on the way out."

"Sure."

Kier disappeared into the kitchen as Danny entered his room and crossed to his closet. He pulled out a duffel, tossed it on the bed, and started grabbing clothes out of the closet, folding them and placing them in packing cubes. Then he headed for his chest of drawers. When he glanced over at his desk, he paused. Had the photo of him and Kier been moved? He frowned and then moved to the bathroom. He started to gather toiletries from the cabinets. He paused when he turned to toss an empty box into the trash can. The bloody bandages were gone, and he damn well hadn't emptied the trash. The beat of his heart sped up.

"Kier? Can you come here? Something's wrong." Danny stood and backed out of the bathroom, bumping into Kier.

"What's wrong?"

"I think someone's been in here."

Kier went still. "Why?"

Danny gripped his arm. "My bandages are gone, and one of my pictures was moved."

Kier's taut muscles relaxed beneath his hand. "Missing trash and a moved picture frame. That's what you're basing your assumption on? Couldn't you have bumped the desk or just that frame? Have you searched through the whole trash can? Maybe the used gauze fell to the bottom." His tone dripped with doubt.

Danny stepped over to the trash can, lifted it, and dumped it on the floor. "No bandages. And I didn't bump the desk."

Kier laid his hands on Danny's shoulders, rubbing them as though attempting to soothe a freaked-out pet. "All right. Let's get your stuff and get out of here. Just to be on the safe side." Kier followed Danny into his room and stopped next to the desk, going very still. "Uh, which of the photos was moved?"

Danny's cheeks warmed as he glanced back at Kier. "The one of us." He studied Kier staring at the image of them smiling into the camera. One of the harried amusement park employees charged with taking group photos as people rush in to conquer roller coasters and churros had taken it. In fact, they'd made him retake it three times.

"I remember that. I had a great time riding the rides at night when they were all lit up by dancing lights." Kier picked up the photo, and a brief smile lifted the corners of his mouth before he schooled his expression. "We look happy, but then both of us had a different idea of where our relationship would go back then." Kier set the photo down and then moved to the window.

Danny went back to packing. His throat burned. "Yeah, I guess you're right. Nothing about our relationship seemed to go as expected."

When Danny had nearly finished, Kier stepped over to the window and peeked through the blinds. Danny's head jerked up when the metal slats snapped closed. Kier rushed to him and started zipping his bag shut.

"We have to go. Now. We'll buy you what you need. Don't ask questions. Just move."

Danny snatched up his laptop as they rushed from the room. They left the same way they entered, which put them out on an exterior walkway that led to the stairs down instead of trapping them on an internal staircase. Danny ran into the back of Kier, who froze in place. He glanced around and saw another individual approach the stairwell. "Shit."

"We're going to have to jump."

Danny's heart pounded, and his breathing sped up. "Are you nuts? I'll break a leg at best, kill myself at worst."

"No, you won't." Danny met Kier's confident gaze. "Trust me."

Danny couldn't speak, couldn't catch his breath. He nodded in response. In a blur Kier disappeared over the railing. Fuck! Danny rushed to the handrail and looked down to find Kier standing on the ground gesturing to him to follow. He dropped his duffel first and then swung one leg over and looked down at Kier, sure and strong and ready to catch him. He braced himself as a wave of nausea rolled through him, but he clenched his stomach muscles, tamping down the sensation. *I must be out of my fucking mind.* The door at the end of the landing opened and an armed man rushed through.

"Stop right there!"

"Dammit, jump!" Kier yelled at him.

As the men raced toward him, Danny stifled a scream as he pushed off the railing and into open air. In a matter of seconds, Kier held him clasped to his chest, but only for a moment before Danny was dumped on his feet. "Move it," Kier barked. His commanding, brook-no-arguments tone got Danny moving. They stayed under cover as they rushed toward the car.

"There's no way we're going to get to the car without them seeing us and likely shooting at us," Danny said.

Kier pulled out his key fob and started his car. "Give me your bag." In a blink, he disappeared from his spot next to Danny and reappeared next to the car. He tossed the bag in the passenger seat and jumped in. He gunned the engine and hopped the curb up onto the grass, pulling up right next to Danny. A shot whizzed by Danny's head. He glanced back to find another of the fatigue-clad men charging toward him.

"Get the hell in the car."

Danny yanked open the door and dove into the back seat.

Kier stomped on the gas and the car raced away from the building.

"Who the hell are they?" asked Danny

"My guess, Purity. By the way, you were right. Someone was definitely in your apartment, and he was still watching it."

Danny scanned the street behind them looking for a tail. Not that he'd know how to spot one.

"They saw me look out the window and they immediately exited their cars and approached the building. They didn't strike me as cops. Only other option is Purity."

His racing heart pounded as Danny fought to breathe. "Why?" He wheezed out the word, then stopped and sucked in a few breaths, attempting to calm himself. When he settled enough to speak, he tried again, turning wide eyes on Kier. "Why? What on earth could Purity want with me? I'm not a vampire, and sending that many people does not imply they just wanted to check on my well-being. So why?"

Kier met Danny's eyes in the rearview mirror. "I don't know, but I promise you they're going to have to go through me to get to you."

DANNY CONTINUED to check over his shoulder until Kier pulled into the garage behind his house and shut the door.

"What the hell was that? Seriously, I don't understand any of this. First, I'm attacked, then my apartment is broken into, then some sort of death squad comes after us, guns blazing." Danny rushed into Kier's house, needing the safety it offered. They made their way down to the main living area. As soon as Danny reached the living room, he immediately started to pace. Kier dropped onto a couch and stretched his long legs out in front of him. He lay his head on the back of the couch and closed his eyes.

"I don't even... I just...." Danny dragged a hand over his face. "Christ. We could have been killed. We could have been kidnapped and taken who knows where, probably never to be heard from again." He plopped down next to Kier. "I feel like the French woman in the first Jason Bourne movie. Especially after you did all that cloak-and-dagger stuff with the car swap." What should have been a twenty-minute drive took more than an hour. Kier drove through streets of Sinclair, traveling down residential roads onto more crowded thoroughfares and back again. They'd left Kier's SUV in a public parking lot and switched over to a plain black sedan. Kier had called a friend as they drove, who left the car in the lot for him. "Do you really think they put a locator on the car?"

Kier lifted his head and met Danny's eyes. Strength and determination shone in the depths of his pale blue gaze. "I have no idea, but it wasn't a chance I was willing to take. Think about it. They were watching your place, waiting for you. There's no other explanation for how they got there so soon after we did, which means they were already there and likely saw us pull up. They know exactly what I drive. It would have been a simple matter for them to put a beacon on the car. They let us get away too easily. It's as though they knew they'd be able to find you."

"Easily! They shot at us."

"With tranq darts. I don't think they wanted us dead. Well, they didn't want you dead. What I want to know is why Purity wants you."

"Purity. Jesus." Something nasty and acrid burned its way up Danny's throat and left a foul taste in his mouth. "Damn." He rubbed his damp palms on his pants. "Is—is this what it's like for you? For all the vampires? Constantly afraid that Purity is going to come gunning for you?" He stepped toward Kier.

"Kind of. The thing with Purity is that despite their 'we're here to protect the public' message, they really aren't. At the core of the group is fear and hatred. If something or someone is even remotely connected to vampires, Purity wants to track it, capture it, maybe study it, but definitely eradicate it. This is why most vampires keep low profiles. It's why revealing ourselves even to people we care about is a huge risk."

Danny sat next to Kier. "God, I can't image living like that." He reached out and laid a hand on Kier's knee. "I'm sorry. I didn't understand. Until now."

They gazed into each other's eyes. Heat spread through Danny, and the air seemed thicker than it had been a moment before. "So, uh, now what?" His voice came out as a thick rasp.

"I think after the last few days you may need a night of normal." Kier laid a hand over Danny's. Heat spread from that point of contact. Danny's heart rate picked up as he studied Kier's gorgeous face. He resisted the urge to reach out and touch Kier's face. He missed his touch, his kiss, how warm and wanted Kier could make him feel. He wanted it back.

"What did you have in mind?"

"We go to work."

"Work? The library?"

"No. The bar. I've got to open tonight. Your job is to stay in my office and out of trouble."

"You're kidding me. You want me to stay cooped up in your office all night? Why don't I just stay here? I'll be out of sight and out of trouble."

"Can't take the chance that somehow they tracked us here. Can't risk you being alone if they should get in or if something goes wrong with your health." Kier linked their fingers. "I need you close—just in case." Their gazes locked, held. For a moment Danny couldn't breathe. Then Kier shifted his eyes away. "So, you get to come experience the wonderful world of bar management. I can do what I need to do and keep you in earshot at the same time. It's a win-win."

"For who?" Even though being stuck in Kier's office all night sounded like the epitome of boring, he'd still be with Kier. His stomach grumbled.

"Come on. Sounds like it's strawberry milkshake time." Kier pushed to his feet and headed for the fridge behind the bar.

"That's not funny, McCade."

"It's a little funny."

Danny rolled his eyes and fought back a smile. Charming bastard. Kier always knew just how to make him smile. He'd missed that during their separation. Hell, he'd just missed Kier. He watched Kier mix his drink; he shook it up like a margarita, putting a little flair into it. He reminded him a bit of that old Tom Cruise movie *Cocktail*, especially when he cracked open the shaker and drained the contents into a highball glass. Then he dug out a tiny umbrella and garnished the drink with it.

"Sorry, I'm fresh out of maraschino cherries."

Danny smiled as he rose and crossed to claim his drink. He sipped and watched Kier clean up the used items. He'd made a mistake running scared. He could see that now that he'd experienced a little bit of what Kier faced every day. And he'd been blind rejecting a good man, one who would stand beside him despite everything, one who could make him tingle. God, he could kick himself, but he wouldn't waste a second chance.

If Purity didn't haul him away to their compound and the changes to his system didn't kill him, he'd put everything into re-earning Kier's trust and winning him back.

# CHAPTER 6

KIER'S BAR, the Haven, occupied a large corner lot about a block away from Kier's house. After taking time to eat, shower, and change, Danny and Kier walked the short distance to the tall brick building to open for the evening. Kier unlocked the door and stepped in. Danny followed and stood just inside the entrance as he waited for Kier to flip on the house lights. In the full bright light, everything looked polished and well maintained, but he wouldn't expect anything less of Kier's place. The door opened again and the opening shift crew trooped into the bar, all offering waves and words of greeting, and then got busy with their individual job duties.

Danny turned back to Kier. "So, what can I do to help?"

"Why don't you come sit in the office? I've got paperwork to do."

Danny frowned. "Can't I help out here? I agree that a night of normal is what I need. Your people are here with me, so I won't be alone. I'll stay out of their way. I promise."

Kier studied him for a long moment. Danny would have paid good money to know what thoughts danced through his mind. "All right, if you want something to do, follow me." Kier walked behind the bar.

Danny followed but stayed on the opposite side. Propping his elbows on the bar and leaning in toward Kier, he asked, "What have you got for me?"

Kier slapped a damp rag and a bucket of soapy water in front of Danny. "I need you to give all of the tables and the bar surface a wipe down with soapy water. Once the doors open and the patrons start arriving, I'll need you to make sure that the tables get cleared and wiped down between parties. Okay?" With that he put an empty plastic tub on the bar.

Danny eyed the bucket, then Kier.

"Is this a problem for you?" Kier shot him a hard stare. "I know this isn't what you're used to, but hey, it's something useful to do."

Danny cocked his head. "You really don't think much of me, do you?"

Kier frowned at him. "What are you talking about?"

"You must think I'm a spoiled brat or pampered or something. I thought you knew me better than that."

"I thought I did, too, but then I got a nasty surprise six months ago. That's when I learned we really didn't know each other at all."

"Kier, dammit."

Kier dropped his chin to his chest. "Shit. I'm sorry."

"It's okay. And you're not wrong. We only knew what we wanted the other to know. We're going to need to work on changing that."

Kier dragged a hand through his hair. "You don't have to pretend you care just to get my help. I think I've already proven that I'm in this until the end."

"I'm not pretending just to get something from you. Give me time. I'll prove it to you." Danny reached out and put a hand on Kier's arm.

Kier looked down at where they connected; then he stepped back out of range. "I've got paperwork to attend to and a bar to open for the evening."

"I'll let you get to it. I've got work to do myself. I'll be just fine out here cleaning and clearing tables. I'll be the best damn busboy you've ever seen."

"We'll see about that." Kier gave him a small smile, then headed back to his office.

Danny stared after him, watching him disappear down the hallway, enjoying the view of the firm curve of Kier's butt, the sexy roll of his hips as he walked away. Heat pooled deep inside. Kier affected him like no other.

He looked around the bar at Kier's friends and employees, most of them likely vampires. Time to start proving to Kier that he'd changed.


"WHAT DO you mean you lost him?" Rogan adjusted his hands-free device on his ear, then coded in to the rear entrance of the Purity compound. He made his way down the main hallway to the entrance to the stairwell.

"I'm sorry, sir, but he wasn't alone."

"Then why the hell did you move on him? Why didn't you wait until he was alone?" He jogged down the stairs and shoved through the door one level down. He stalked down the cinder block hallway toward his office.

"We got a message from Ms. Moran that we were to apprehend the man at the first opportunity. This was the first time he came back to his apartment all day."

*Fucking Melissa.* He shoved into his office. The door slapped against the concrete wall. He stopped in the middle of his office, pressed his fingers to his eyes.

"Sir, are you still there?"

"Yeah." He blew out a breath and started pacing.

"Who was he with?"

"A vampire."

"What?" Rogan stopped.

"Yes. It has to be. Only a vamp can move the way that guy did."

"Well, fuck." Rogan jammed a hand on his hips. He shoulders slumped forward.

"It gets worse. They had a suitcase with them. I don't think the target plans to come back to his apartment anytime soon."

"Double fuck." Rogan's head dropped back, and he gazed blindly at the ceiling. "Melissa is going to be beyond pissed."

"Melissa is going to be beyond pissed about what?"

Shit. Rogan's body tensed. He made a slow pivot toward the entrance to his office to find Melissa standing there, hands clasped behind her back, an eyebrow raised at him.

"Do we have him yet?"

Rogan held up a finger to halt further questioning, then continued to pace. "Where are you now?"

"We're still searching the neighborhood. We lost track of the car. We got a tracker on the car they arrived in, but at some point they switched vehicles. There is still a team on the apartment, but they report that the place is quiet."

Rogan pinched the bridge of his nose. "Come on back in. I'm going to send a fresh team out to sit on the apartment overnight and the car. They'll have to come back to one or the other eventually."

"Yes, sir."

Rogan tapped the button on the earpiece and disconnected the call. "Shit." He dragged a hand through his hair.

"Rogan. Do. We. Have. Him."

"No." Rogan shoved his hands in his pockets and waited.

Her tone dropped the temperature in the room by five degrees. "Why the hell not?"

"He wasn't alone. He had someone with him who helped him get away from us."

"Who?"

"We don't know. Maybe a vampire."

"Were your men not equipped to deal with a single vampire and a human?"

"My men were more than prepared." Rogan gritted his teeth.

She snorted. "All evidence to the contrary." She whirled and strode out of the office. "I'm surrounded by incompetence. Have to do everything myself."

"What does that mean?" Rogan got no response. The hair rose on the back of his neck. Something told him to go after her.

He followed Melissa, at a discreet distance, into the stairwell and down to the basement level of the building. The quiet ranting started again once she shoved through the doors and into the gray concrete hallway of the sub-basement. Warning bells sounded in Rogan's head. No one came down here except for the facilities crew. Purity used this floor for storage of old files and extra supplies, nothing more. Melissa didn't need anything down here. Even if she did she wouldn't get it herself, she'd send a minion.

She rounded a corner. Not knowing what to expect, Rogan eased his way to the end of the hall, staying as quiet as possible and using the rumble of the heating system to cover his approach. He edged around the corner just enough to catch sight of Melissa disappearing through a heavy metal door. Rogan rushed forward, but not in time to catch it before it shut and locked behind her. Dammit.

He studied the combination pad and gave serious consideration to getting some fingerprint powder or something to help him figure out the code to the door. He tabled that idea for the moment. That task would be best saved until Melissa's day off, when he'd have more time to clean up after himself without fear of discovery. He searched the stretch of hallway surrounding the door looking for added layers of security or alternate entrances and found nothing.

*What are you hiding down here?* Rogan studied the door one last time before heading back toward the stairs. Something told Rogan he needed to watch her like a hawk. She was planning something. Something big, and she kept it hidden behind that door. Nothing good ever came from Melissa Moran having a secret. An entire room full of secrets could be disastrous.

A FEW hours into his first shift as a busboy, Danny wanted to retire from his career in the food service industry.

"Danny, table one needs clearing."

He groaned. He'd enjoyed his little trip into normalcy, but he wanted to go back to the land of books and paperwork. But he'd settle for whatever would keep him from lugging one more load of dishes.

Still, he'd asked for this, promised he'd give it his best. With a sigh, he stopped loading the half-full dishwasher, grabbed his rag and a tub, and trudged over to wipe up spilled beer and collect more dirty mugs and plates that needed to be cleaned.

He slapped the damp cloth on the table and wiped it clean. When he finished, he hefted the bin of dirty glasses and moved to the next table. "I have a master's degree. I had a successful career as a librarian."

"Problems, Book Boy?"

Danny glanced up, and his gaze connected with the amused green eyes of the bartender, Alex. "Book Boy?"

She shrugged. "Seemed appropriate. Missing your job playing with musty old books?" The pink-haired bartender in a Metallica tank top gave him a once-over as she pulled a mug of beer for a patron who'd just claimed a seat at the bar a moment before.

"Yes. I really am."

She laughed, finished serving the man, and then dried her hands on a dish towel. She nodded toward the back hall. "Come on. Let's take a quick break."

Danny smiled, appreciating the offer and the promise of a chair. He followed her down the hallway past Kier's office. Danny peeked in as they passed. Kier sat behind his desk sorting through stacks of papers, his brows furrowed in concentration.

They stopped just inside the rear entrance and cracked the door to let in air. The blast of cold was a blessing. With wall-to-wall patrons, the temperature inside the Haven had risen fast.

"So, you want to tell me what's going on? Kier wasn't exactly forthcoming earlier when he called and said he needed to borrow a car." Alex pulled out a pack of gum, offered a stick, then selected a piece for herself when Danny declined.

"What do you mean?"

"Don't play games with me. We both know you're no idiot. You've got a master's degree, right?" She smirked at him.

"Heard that, did you?" Danny grimaced.

"I've got good ears. Most vampires do."

"Really? Do you mean you can hear things humans can't, or was that just an expression?"

"Most vampires have exceptional hearing. When you're bitching under your breath, most of the bar can hear you loud and clear."

"Well, shit. Nice impression." His cheeks heated. He'd been whining under his breath for the better part of a half an hour.

"You know what other exceptional senses I've got?"

"I'm guessing sight."

"Bingo. Let me tell you what I see. I see my best friend spending a heck of a lot of time with a man who ripped out his heart. A man who, to be honest, I never really expected and sort of hoped I wouldn't see again." She leaned into him and poked him in the chest. "You had him all but floating. Then you shoved him off that cloud in the most heartless way possible. I'm not going to let you hurt him again. So, spill. What the hell is going on, Danny?"

Danny scanned the woman before him. His gaze took in her tense posture, her clenched fists, and settled on brilliant green eyes that gleamed with determination. He'd gotten to know her a little over the course of the half year he and Kier had dated. He liked her, her toughness and her fierce protectiveness of Kier. He never thought he'd be on the business end of that protective nature, though.

"I'm in a little bit—okay, a lot of trouble, and I didn't know where else to turn. I'm not prepared to get into the details of it all right now."

"Uh-huh."

Danny swallowed when Alex's fangs slid down over her lip.

"If he gets hurt, or worse killed, because of you, you will not like the consequences. Are we clear?"

Danny nodded and crossed his arms as his stomach clenched. "You know I never meant to hurt him."

She snorted out a laugh. "Well, you did. I've known Kier for at least a hundred years—"

Danny's jaw dropped. "A hundred years?"

"Didn't have that conversation yet, huh?"

"We did. Doesn't make it any less shocking." Danny shoved his hands in his pocket and shivered as the cold of the night overcame the heat in the bar. "As to the rest, we're working our way through it all. But then, we've had a rather eventful few days. Can I ask, how exactly did you two meet?"

"You really want to talk about that now?"

"I'm trying to learn more about Kier, about his friends, about vampires in general. Talking to one of his oldest friends seems like a good jumping-off point."

"Fair. Let's just say I'd gotten myself into a little bit of a tough spot and Kier came to my rescue."

"When was this?"

"London 1915."

"During World War I?"

"That's right, Book Boy, and that's all you need to know."

"Are you the same age?"

"Roughly."

"Did you ever—?"

"No. We were and always will be friends. I probably know him better than anyone else. That's why I can say without a doubt that I've never seen him as gone over anyone as he was over you or as crushed as when you walked away." She held his gaze as she stepped back from him and leaned against the opposite wall.

Danny couldn't draw a full breath, and a lump formed in his throat. He hated that he'd hurt him like that.

"Look, I can respect that you don't want to get into the details of your relationship with me, just don't do that to him again. Figure out if you're willing to accept who and what he is, because if he's hurt again... let's just say you won't like me very much. Clear?"

Danny responded in a quiet voice. "Clear."

"Good." Alex smiled, releasing the intensity of the moment before. "You ready to get back to it?"

"No, but let's do it anyway."

Something slammed in Kier's office. Danny pushed off the wall, but Alex stopped him with a hand on his arm. "It's best to stay clear of the office while Kier's tangling with the monthly accounting."

Another crash burst from Kier's office, and a second later he appeared in the hall, a tuft of hair sticking out to the side. He blinked when he caught sight of Alex and Danny. Kier shot Alex a questioning glance as he walked toward them.

"You okay? We heard some banging coming from in there," Danny asked, laying a hand on his arm.

"That was me banging my head against the wall. I hate going over the books."

"Don't you have an accountant to handle this?"

"I do, but he's been on vacation for about a month and I didn't want to let things sit that long. Is everything all right out here?"

"Yep. We just needed to take a short break. Cool off. Things have settled down a little, so we came to get a little air." Alex smiled and laid a hand on Kier's shoulder.

Kier raised a brow at Danny.

"Everything's fine. I'm just not used to this level of manual labor." He forced a laugh, then shivered. Kier reached out and pulled the back door shut.

"I was just saying hello to Danny. Catching up, getting a good whiff of him. It was quite a surprise to see him here after all these months. Call me crazy, but I think there's something different about him. His scent is off."

"Different is putting it mildly." Danny muttered the words under his breath. "Wait, did you say whiff? Don't do that. Human or vampire, going around sniffing people is just weird."

Alex rolled her eyes. "You'll get used to it. It's part of the culture."

"If you say so." Danny shook his head.

Alex locked eyes with Kier as she reached out and gripped his shoulder. "Since he won't—" She lifted her chin toward Danny. "—I'm asking you to be straight up with me, K. Why's he here? What's wrong with him?" She held up a hand when Kier started to speak. "Don't bullshit me. I've known you too long for that mess. Truth. I can't watch out for either of you if I don't know what's going on."

Kier hesitated and looked at Danny, his expression asking for permission.

Danny sighed. "Tell her."

She studied Danny with the laser-sharp gaze of a scientist looking through a microscope. Then her eyes went wide. "He's been turned, hasn't he?" She went several shades paler then her usual pasty complexion. "Good God, Kier, what the hell have you two done? Do you know the type of attention this could bring on us? I mean, I like Danny for the most part, but did you really need to turn your ex? You couldn't find a nice vampire to settle down with?"

"Shut up, Alex. He hasn't been turned exactly, and I'm certainly not the cause of his current condition."

"Then who is?"

Kier's voice went quiet. "Rogue vampire attacked Danny. I think Purity did something to him. From how Danny describes him, it sounds like something wasn't right with this vamp. I've taken him to see Sharon. Based on the blood tests she's run, something was definitely wrong with this guy and whatever it is has affected Danny. The vampire is dead now."

"Shit, Kier. You do realize the world of hurt you're going to bring down on yourself if Purity is involved. They won't stop looking for you two. Is that why I dropped a car off for you earlier?"

Kier drew in a breath and gave her the quick and dirty rundown of everything that had happened in the last few days. When he finished, Alex gripped his arm. "Promise me you'll be careful. Don't draw attention to yourself, and avoid Purity at all costs. I don't want to see you hurt, for any reason." Her gaze flicked toward Danny.

"Alex, I know what I'm doing." He pulled her into a tight hug. They rocked together for a few moments, then separated.

"Why don't we all just get back to work and put all of this aside for the night. Okay?" Kier patted Alex's shoulder, nodded at Danny, and then headed back for his office. When Kier disappeared through the doorway and shut it behind him, Alex turned to Danny. "I'm sorry for everything that you're going through right now, but if anything happens to him…."

"I know. I know. You and I are going to have a problem."

Alex turned, rolled her shoulders, and headed back out into the bar.

"So much for normal," Danny muttered, then headed into the crowd and noise of the bar to lose himself in work.


KIER STOOD in the shadows of the hallway and studied Danny as he worked. It still rattled him to have Danny back in his life. In all this time, the lithe blond man with the striking brown eyes still managed to take up a remarkable amount of his mental real estate. With his hair disheveled and his cheeks a touch flush from exertions and irritation, he reminded Kier of how he'd looked after their first kiss. *Don't go there. Don't pick the scab.* Try as he might, he couldn't manage to fend off the memory of Danny with hair tousled from Kier running his fingers through it, pink, kiss-swollen lips, shirt open revealing a firm, smooth chest. His eyes shined as he wrapped his arms around Kier and pulled him close. He'd been all but drunk off the taste of Danny, and he'd never wanted to sober up. Kier fought for breath under the weight of the memory. He reached up and rubbed at the ache in his chest.

Glutton for punishment, he went back to watching Danny as he moved through the room chatting with patrons and never noticing the odd looks he got from some in the crowd. Chances were people either knew of their past relationship or they caught Danny's not-quite-a-vampire scent.

"Still think you know what you're doing?"

Kier jerked. He hadn't noticed Alex leaning in the stockroom doorway, arms crossed and a frown on her face.

"Jesus, Alex. Make noise next time."

"A whole drum line could have paraded around you and you wouldn't have noticed. You were too lost in the box full of drama currently cleaning up your main room."

"He's only here because he needs help. What do you want me to do, turn my back, leave him to fend for himself in a world he knows nothing about?"

"Kier, come on. It's me. I know you. I saw what Danny's leaving did to you. Why would you open yourself up to it again?"

"I'm not. I'm just helping him."

Alex snorted. "You keep telling yourself that. Maybe one day we'll both believe it. That wound has just barely scabbed over, and now you go and pick it. I get it. You're a good guy and you can't leave a friend in need twisting in the wind, but what about you? Who's going to look after you?"

"That's what I've got you here for." Kier lightly bumped shoulders with Alex.

"You know I'll always be here for you, but you've got to help me out. Tell me honestly, is he going to stay this time?"

Kier closed his eyes, swiped a hand down his face. "I don't know. It's complicated."

"Are you going to turn him?"

"Only if I have to. This condition of his may leave me with no choice."

"Do you know if he even wants to be turned? What if he'd rather die than live as a vampire?"

The thought stole his breath, made his chest tighten. Alex put a hand on his shoulder. When he met her eyes, she gave him a knowing smile. Even if he wasn't ready to open himself up to Danny again, Kier didn't know how he'd face a world without him in it. Once upon a time Kier thought he'd shared a link with Danny. He thought they'd be connected in every way, mind, body, and soul. Something deep inside clenched at the thought of that never happening. No matter how hard his head resisted, a small piece of his heart still longed.

"I don't know if I can give him that choice. I can't stand by and watch him die when I can do something about it, and considering how he feels about vampires, that would be it for us. He'd hate me for eternity, but at least he'd be alive." Kier squeezed his eyes shut.

"So, you'll have a connection to a man who detests you for the rest of your life. You'll never be able to make a clean break from him. It's been six months and you still have feelings for him."

"And I will find a way to deal with them. We've both been around for a long time. We've both had loss, and we've both learned how to deal with that pain and loss. Trust me. I will be all right, but I love you for trying to protect me."

He hoped he would, at any rate. He'd tried to convince himself that he'd moved beyond Danny. Then he'd turn around and see a picture, hear a song, or smell an aroma that brought a memory of them together careening back. How the hell do you get over someone when every damn thing reminds you of them?

"My relationship with Danny will be like that of master and apprentice. As soon as I equip Danny to stand on his own two feet as a vampire, I'll help find him a job, one more suited for a person with Danny's education, and a place to live. Then he's on his own. I'll, of course, do my duty as his master should he need me, but that's it. That's where it ends. It has to."

Alex started looking around on the floor and checking her shoes. "What?"

"Trying to watch where I'm standing because the bullshit is getting deep in here. You're about as likely to walk away from Danny as I am to do a striptease on the bar. Danny is special to you. Has been since the day you met and always will be."

Kier shifted his gaze back to Danny. He watched him lug another bunch of empty glasses back to the bar, and a tingle went through him as he skimmed his gaze over the flexing muscles of Danny's back as he carried the heavy tub. The T-shirt Kier had given Danny clung to him, and the jeans hugged the curves of his firm ass. Kier forced himself to tear his gaze away. Damn Alex for knowing him so well.

She was right. The longer Danny stayed around, the more Kier would start breaking his vow to keep his distance. Hell, it had already started. Every wall Kier built, Danny somehow scaled it.

Alex whacked his chest with the back of her hand, drawing him out of his thoughts. "If I don't miss my guess, there's still feeling there for Reynolds too." She tipped her chin toward Danny, who'd snagged a stool and a bottle of water. He sat, chatting with some of the bar patrons as though he hung out with vampires all the time. "I think he's trying, K. For you."

"I don't know. Maybe."

"Have you two talked at all?"

"We've started to. Things have been kind of crazy."

"No more excuses, McCade. Man up. Work your shit out. Don't waste the opportunity that's been handed to you. Stop hiding behind the shields you're so good at erecting."

Alex walked away, leaving Kier watching Danny interacting with his friends and customers, trying to fit into his world. But could he trust this change of heart? Could he risk his heart and open it to Danny Reynolds again?

# CHAPTER 7

"I'D LIKE to state for the record that you suck. Did you enjoy making me busboy for the evening?" Danny trudged into Kier's living room, kicked off his shoes, and flopped on the couch. He let himself sink into the soft, deep cushions with a long groan. The grandfather clock in the hallway chimed three o'clock.

"You didn't have to do it, you know. It's not like I'm your boss. You don't have to pay me in trade for helping you."

Danny scratched the back of his neck, and then he held out a hand. When Kier crossed to him and took the offered hand, Danny tugged him down next to him. Swiveling to face him, Danny took Kier's face in his hands and locked eyes with him. "I'm going to say this one more time, and I want you to hear me, okay?"

Kier nodded.

"I don't do anything I don't want to do. While I am grateful for your help with my current predicament, I don't feel obligated to offer myself up as laborer. I am going to be spectacularly sore tomorrow. Why would I put up with that if I didn't want to?"

Kier started to answer, but Danny covered his lips with two fingers. "I wanted to help. I liked helping in your bar. I liked meeting your friends. Don't make me say it again."

The corner of Kier's mouth quirked up. "Understood."

Danny flopped back on the couch. "I could get used to this, working at the bar."

Kier raised an eyebrow at him.

"I'm not saying I'm looking to make a total career change, but it's a fun contrast to working in the library." Danny looked at Kier, who'd sprawled back on the couch but continued to watch him.

The man looked sexy as hell with his dark hair a bit mussed, his black long-sleeve tee hugging every well-toned muscle in his arms and stretching across his chest. He sat with his thighs spread just enough so Danny could admire the way the denim cupped the bulge of his crotch. For a moment time ceased to exist, and nothing mattered but this beautiful man and this moment. His heart rate sped up; a low, simmering heat ignited in him. He wanted to reach out and touch the warm skin. Taste the warm, rich flavor of his lips.

Danny shook his head to clear it and shifted in his seat, unable to settle. Energy pulsed through his body. He should've been exhausted, not ready to run laps around the block or better yet jump on Kier until he burned out.

Danny cleared his throat and took a few slow breaths. "So, what now? Late-night movies, a little music and wine to mellow out?"

"Now, I go to bed. I'm beat." Kier pushed up out of the chair. "Do you have everything you need for the night? Are you hungry?"

"I'm good, but I am a bit wired. Sometimes watching movies I've already seen helps me relax and fall asleep. I'm assuming you've got someplace I can do that down here." Danny glanced around the room, searching for a television.

"Come with me. I think you'll like this." Kier laid a hand on his back, then went still and moved his hand to Danny's forehead. "You're a little warm. How are you feeling?"

"I am?" Danny pressed the back of his hand to his cheek. "I feel fine. A bit keyed up, but otherwise I feel great."

Kier frowned but guided him to another room.

Kier led Danny into the entertainment room of his dreams. Danny froze in the doorway, and pleasure bubbled up inside him as he took in a space chock-full of comfy chairs and all of the latest gadgets and consoles.

"Wow. Christmas came early this year."

Danny rushed into the room and tried to inspect everything all at once. He never noticed Kier leave the room and come back with pillows and blankets.

"Are we having a sleepover?"

Kier chuckled. "No, but I figured these would make you more comfortable if you fall asleep in here."

"Good plan. I knew I kept you around for a reason."

"Uh, thanks—I think."

Danny took the bedding, set up one of the recliners just how he wanted it, picked a movie, and then handed it to Kier. "Are you sure I can't talk you into watching a movie with me?" he asked as he snuggled in, ready for explosions and adventure.

Kier shook his head. "I'll get you set up before I head to bed."

Danny tamped down a flicker of disappointment.

Kier got the system up and running, then handed Danny the remote. He touched his hand to his forehead one more time.

"Are you sure you're feeling well?"

Danny reached out and laid a hand on Kier's arm. "Yes. Never better."

Kier scanned his face once more, concern flashing in his eyes.

"If you need anything, just call for me."

"Yes, yes. I will. Go to bed. Sleep well."

Kier nodded, then headed for the door.

Danny watched him walk out of the room. A minute later, Danny clenched the arms of the reclining chair as the room spun. His entire body broke out into a cold sweat, and he began to shiver violently. Danny's heart hammered, and breath raced in and out of his lungs. As he pushed up from the chair, a blinding pain slammed into him. His knees buckled and he hit the floor.


"KIER!"

At Danny's agonized cry, Kier rushed back into the den in a blur of speed. He found Danny curled on the floor, writhing in pain.

"What happened? What's wrong? Talk to me, Danny." Kier knelt at Danny's side. Heat pumped off Danny's flushed skin. He reached out to touch, but his hands hovered, then clenched. He didn't know if touching him would help or cause him more pain.

"Kier." Danny gasped and snagged his hand, his grip tighter than normal for a human. Terror and agony shone in Danny's wide brown eyes.

Kier cradled Danny to him, at a complete loss. "I knew something was wrong. Dammit, I should have called Sharon the minute I noticed your fever and had her come check on you."

Danny rolled on his side and buried his face in Kier's lap, clenched his hands in his shirt. "God, make it stop. Please." Danny moaned, his breathing hissing out. Kier stroked his hands through Danny's hair. "God, Kier. What's happening to me?"

"I don't know, love. But I'm going to get you help. We're going to fix this. Try to slow your breathing a little." He kept his tone calm and even as sweat rolled down his back and his hands trembled. He eased Danny back down onto the rug and pushed up to his feet.

Danny's hand latched on to his ankle, his grip vise-tight. "Don't leave me."

He knelt and cupped Danny's cheek. "I'm not going far. I need my phone. I left it in my bedroom. You hang tight. I'll be back before you know it."

"No, please." Danny's voice broke, and Kier's gut clenched at the scared, desperate sound.

"Dan, I've got to call Sharon. She's the only one with a shot at making you better right now." He eased his leg from Danny's grip and put his preternatural speed to good use. He made it to his bedroom and back in a flash. He fisted his hand, released it, then shook it out to stop the fine tremor that had set in. He swiped to unlock his phone, then jabbed at the screen, grateful for favorites and speed dial. Sitting on the floor, he pulled Danny to him so that he could cradle his head in his lap again. He growled under his breath as he waited for a response. "Answer the phone, dammit. Come on, Sharon. Where the hell are you?"

"Hello to you too. If you must know, I was in my lab. What can I do for you, oh impatient one?"

"You've got to get over here. Something's wrong with Danny."

"What are his symptoms?" She shifted into doctor mode without even pausing. A small bubble of relief floated up in Kier.

"Pain. He's in a lot of pain. He's burning up."

"Dizzy." Danny moaned and Kier rubbed Danny's chest.

"Walk me through it. When was the onset?"

"We'd just gotten home. He seemed a little fidgety but fine. Just before I headed to bed, I noticed he felt a little hot. I hadn't been out of the room for more than thirty seconds when I heard him yell my name. I came back and he was on the floor writhing in pain. I don't know what to do for him. You've got to help me, Shar."

"Okay, just stay calm. We'll figure this out."

Kier clenched his jaw. He hated this. Hated to see Danny suffer, hated that he had nothing more to offer than comfort. He couldn't just sit here listening to every whimper and groan. Each pained sound out of Danny hit him like a hammer to the chest.

"God, Kier, make this stop. Please." Danny's agony-filled eyes met his.

Kier opened his mouth to speak, then closed it and just growled. He had nothing. No answers, no solutions. He pinned the phone between his ear and his shoulder and reached out to take Danny into his arms. "What's happening to him, Sharon?"

"It's possible his condition is progressing. Keir, I think the vampire that attacked Danny was genetically manipulated. It's possible that his attacker's blood is still attempting to convert him, but the problem is that whatever was done to that vamp weakened his blood. So it was powerful or different enough to trigger a process that never should have gotten started with such a small quantity of blood consumed. Plus, it's making the conversion process drawn out and excruciating."

"What the hell does that mean?" he barked.

"It's almost like they were trying to figure out how to change a vampire back into a regular human."

A chill ran through Kier. His voice went low and quiet. "Purity?"

"Probably."

He glanced down at Danny curled into the fetal position in Kier's lap, his whole body shaking.

"Fuck. Okay, enough with the science lesson. What do I need to do for Danny right now?"

"I don't know for sure, Kier. I'm still studying this. We can try getting some of your blood into him. A little pure vampire blood might counteract the effects of the tainted blood."

"I'm pretty sure he doesn't want to be turned."

"We both know a true conversion takes more than just a tiny bit of blood. Just try it. I can't see it hurting anything. Honestly, Kier, I'm flying blind here, but during initial conversion the fledgling needs to ingest pure vampire blood multiple times. Danny hasn't had any since the attack, and that definitely wasn't pure blood."

"Would more of the mixture that we've been giving him help?"

"Maybe, but I'm guessing warm and straight from the source would be better. Sort of like the difference between giving a drug by IV versus orally."

Kier eyed Danny, not sure how he would respond to this suggestion. "Hold on a sec." He set the phone down and cupped Danny's chin, encouraging him to look at him. "Dan, I want you to drink some of my blood."

Danny wrinkled his nose. "Why?"

"Sharon thinks it might help. She thinks pure blood might make a difference. Just a little. Not enough to turn you. I promise."

Danny buried his face against Kier's chest and said nothing. His entire body tensed as a fresh wave of pain rolled through him. "Fine. Let's do this," Danny groaned out as the pain ebbed.

"This better damn well work," Kier muttered. He willed his fangs to lower, bit into his wrist, then offered it to Danny. "Danny, open your eyes. I need you to drink."

Danny cracked open an eye, took one look at the blood oozing from Kier's wrists. He curled tighter into himself for a second, then grabbed Kier and pulled his arm close to his mouth.

He swiped his tongue over the trail of blood. Crinkled his nose.

"God, it's like licking pennies."

"Danny, shut up and drink."

Danny grunted, then placed his mouth over the cut and sucked.

For a brief moment, heat and pleasure overrode panic and worry. For months Kier dreamed of having Danny's mouth on him, drinking from him. The fantasy never involved Danny writhing in pain nor Sharon yelling in his ear. But he wouldn't forget the moment of pure pleasure feeding Danny brought him.

Kier snapped back into the present when Danny started coughing. Kier patted his back. "How are you doing?"

"Stomach feels weird. I don't want to drink any more."

Kier nodded. He licked the wound so it would heal, then pulled Danny tighter to him and just held him. They sat that way for a minute until a small, female voice shouted for him.

"Kier, dammit, pick up the phone. Tell me what's going on."

He snatched his phone up from where he'd dropped it on the carpet and hit the speaker button. "Sharon, I'm here."

"How's Danny?"

He stroked Danny's head, his arm, his hip. With each stroke, tension drained from Danny's body. His muscles started to relax, and his breathing slowed. Heat no longer poured off him, and his trembling slowed to a stop.

"He's better. It seems to be working." He blew out a long, slow breath. *Thank God.* Kier closed his eyes and took a few steadying breaths to calm his own system. "Do you think I should bring him over to see you?"

"No. I'll come to you. I want him to rest for now, but I do want to look him over and take some fresh blood samples. We need to see if his blood is changing, and if so, how."

"Good idea." He closed his eyes, breathed out. "I'll see you in a bit, Sharon. Just come to the rear entrance."

"You got it. Call me if anything changes." Kier disconnected the call, dropped the phone, and just sat holding Danny. A second later his eyes shot back open when Danny clutched his thigh. Danny had gone chalk white, sweat ran down his face, and his dark chocolate eyes flared wide.

"Bathroom. Now." That's all he got out before slapping a hand over his mouth. Kier scooped him up, and in a blur of movement, whisked him down the hall and into the bathroom in time for Danny to be violently ill. When he finished, Danny slumped onto the floor. He placed his forehead against the porcelain toilet bowl as shivers racked his body.

Kier filled a small cup with water and handed it to Danny, who rinsed his mouth out, then held the cup aloft for more. After chugging three cups of cold water, he rolled his head so that his temple still pressed to the cool bowl. "Shoot me now. It's more merciful than forcing me to go through more of this."

"Just hang in there, Dan. We'll get whatever this is figured out. Stay here. I'm going to get you a change of clothes and call Sharon again. Do you still feel sick, or do you want to go lie down?"

Danny closed his eyes for a moment. "I think I'm okay. The pain, the sickness, the shakes, it's all gone. All I want to do now is sleep."

Danny's shoulders sagged. He looked tired, sweaty, and defeated. Kier rubbed at the tightness in his chest. He hated seeing Danny this beaten down and vulnerable. Kier bent down, lifted Danny into his arms, and carried him into his bedroom. Moments after he tucked him under the covers, a light snore emitted from Danny.

Kier stared at the pale sleeping face of the beautiful man who he couldn't manage to cut out of his heart. He brushed his fingers over his hair, his cheek. He walked out of the room, pulled the door closed, and braced himself against the wall as his knees went weak. He buried his face in shaking hands and blew out slow, shuddering breaths.

"Shit— Shit." He wiped a hand over his mouth, then sucked in two more breaths before shoving away from the wall. He went to retrieve his phone, snatching it up from where he'd left it, and dropped onto one of the recliners.

He tapped Sharon's number. She picked up in one ring. "What happened?"

"I'm pretty sure he puked up a lung, and I'm not sure how much, if any, of my blood stayed in him, but whatever this was seems to have passed. He's out cold at the moment."

"Stay with him tonight, Kier, just in case this starts again."

"Of course, but I pray to God it doesn't. It kills me to see him like this."

"I know it does, but we'll get him through it."

"How's the research coming? Are we any closer to a fix for this?"

"I wish I had good news for you, but I don't. I've never seen anything like this. If I'm right and his attacker was genetically altered in some way, then I have no way of knowing what's going on in Danny's body. Which means I've got no idea of how long or even if I can find a way to cure him."

Kier's stomach sank. "So what you're saying is that conversion is looking more and more like his only option for survival."

"If I could get more information about what was done to his attacker, maybe I could give you better news. Otherwise, and I hate to say this, we may need to start talking to him about turning."

Kier slumped in his chair. "Fuck."

DANNY AWOKE wrapped in warmth. The awful sickness from last night seemed to be gone and, so far, he had no aftereffects. He expected to at least have sore muscles or a raw stomach, but no. He snuggled in deeper under the thick quilt, opened one eye, and saw a hand. He blinked and realized that his head rested on the solid muscle of Kier's arm. Danny smiled, adjusted again. In response to his slight movements, Kier curled around him, slid his other arm around Danny's stomach, and then pulled him close. He closed his eyes and basked at being in Kier's arms again. He reveled in being pressed tight to his warm, firm body. God, he'd missed this. Missed being held close, missed mornings of lying in Kier's arms. It had taken him weeks, but the first thing he'd admitted to himself after leaving Kier was that he simply missed the man's presence. He missed how just being with Kier could make everything all right.

He turned his head and rolled a bit, trying to see Kier's face. He found stunning blue eyes watching him. Warmth spread through Danny. He smiled, suppressing the urge to roll over so he could stroke his fingers through Kier's thick, dark hair. He wanted to lean up and kiss Kier's soft, full lips. But he couldn't, and he only had himself to blame. Too much movement might bring this magic moment to an end too soon. Instead, he continued to gaze into Kier's eyes and longed to have him the way he used to with desire and care instead of the watchful wariness now present.

"Morning. How do you feel?"

"Hi. I'm feeling well. No remaining ill effects from last night's little adventure whatsoever."

"Good." Kier shifted his gaze away and eased himself into a sitting position. "Scared me last night. I hated seeing you sick and in pain. Sharon came over and checked on you and took more samples. Do you remember any of that?"

Danny shook his head. "I remember the pain, but I also remember drinking your blood. I still kind of have a metal taste in the back of my throat."

Kier stared down at the comforter. "Sorry I had to make you do that, but it may have helped some."

"Honestly, it wasn't bad as I thought it would be, but it's no strawberry shake."

A small smile played about Kier's lips.

"The last thing I remember is you tucking me in bed."

"You were out cold after that. You sort of woke up when Sharon stuck you with the needle, but you dropped back out."

"What did you guys do to fix me?"

"Besides the blood, nothing. After you got sick that last time, it stopped on its own."

"The fact that I got sick after you fed me. Does that mean my special shakes won't sit well anymore?"

"Can't be certain. Sharon thinks you got sick because you already weren't feeling well combined with the taste and texture of straight blood. At this point we have to watch and wait. That's why I'm here. I didn't want to leave you on your own in case something else happened."

"I appreciate it."

"Yeah, well—" Kier swung his leg over the side of the bed.

Before he could stand, Danny put a hand on his shoulder. "I mean it. Thank you for taking care of me."

"You're welcome," Kier said with a nod.

"I—I wanted you to know that I missed this."

"What?"

"I missed being with you like this."

"Well, the physical parts of our relationship were always pretty damn good." Kier blew out a breath. "I need to take a shower." Kier rose and started across the room toward the bathroom.

"That's not what I mean. I miss more than the physical," Danny said. Kier stopped but didn't look back. "Despite everything, I think I just miss you."

Kier looked back over his shoulder. "Why?"

Danny slid over to sit in the place Kier had vacated. He rubbed the silken fabric of the comforter between his fingers. "I guess part of it is proximity. Seeing you again, I'm remembering the good."

"And conveniently forgetting the bad?" Kier's tone stayed level and revealed nothing of his thoughts or emotions.

"No. I just—" Danny shrugged.

Kier turned to face him. "I get it, Dan. I do. You're scared. We have a history. So you feel grateful and it's making you think you have real feelings for me when you don't."

"That's not true. God, please stop assuming you know how I feel." Danny disengaged himself from the tangle of covers and crossed to stand in front of Kier. He reached out to touch him, then balled his fist and let his hand drop. "Come sit with me. I think it's time we lay everything on the table."

Kier raised an eyebrow at him. "You want to do this now? First thing in the morn—" He glanced at the clock; it read three thirty in the afternoon. "First thing after we get up?"

This time Danny did reach out. He hesitated a moment, then placed his hand on Kier's arm. "I do. I want to try and get rid of this underlying awkwardness. I'm hoping that maybe we can try to be friends again. I'll be around for a while to come, I hope, and I think it would be better for both of us to be able to be comfortable around each other again. The longer we let unspoken feelings fester, the worse it will be."

Kier studied him for a long moment. Danny's stomach danced with nerves. Kier had an excellent poker face. "All right. Just let me use the bathroom first. I'll meet you in the kitchen."

Danny gave him a small smile and a nod. He grabbed his jeans off a chest at the foot of the bed and tugged them on. He made his own stop in the bathroom, then headed for the kitchen. He set a pot of coffee brewing. The aroma tormented him, but with the uncertain state of his stomach, he didn't want to risk it.

Kier emerged from his bedroom a few minutes later. He'd tamed his hair from its previously disheveled state, but the night's growth of stubble remained. He still wore the T-shirt he'd slept in but now wore jeans instead of just the light blue boxer briefs. He looked sexy, sleepy, and wary as his gaze flicked to Danny and then over to the coffeepot.

"If you want water—or, well, I guess water since that's the only safe thing for you to ingest—you don't need to wait for me to get it."

"I know. I'm good, thanks." Danny claimed a stool at the kitchen island and then raked a hand through his hair, not sure where to start.

Kier poured his cup, then, despite Danny's protest, grabbed a bottle of water out of the fridge. He set it on the counter in front of Danny before stepping back and leaning against the far counter. "So...."

"Yeah. So.... Cards on the table time. No holding back. Agreed?"

Kier nodded, but still that unreadable expression remained in place. Danny dragged a hand down his face. "I don't know where to start. I guess the night it all went to hell." He flattened his palms against the cool black granite countertop.

"When I found out you were a vampire, suffice it to say the timing and the way I found out sent me into a tailspin."

Kier rubbed the back of his neck. "I was working up the courage to tell you. I never meant for you to find out that way. I just couldn't find the words. I knew you were in that group, and I knew something bad had happened involving a vampire. I didn't know how to tell you I was the very thing that scared you. I hoped that getting to know me would temper your response to the news, make it easier for you to accept." Kier rounded the island and took the stool next to Danny.

"It probably would have, but I had just come to you directly from readmitting my brother to the hospital. I don't know what triggered him that night, but he was in the grips of a massive panic attack. He was reliving his whole ordeal, and nothing I did seemed to help. It took all of us to get him settled and get him an emergency appointment with his psychiatrist. After that, God, I needed you. Then I walk into your office at the bar and find my supposedly human lover drinking blood from some skank."

"Fuck." Kier pressed his fingers to his eyes.

"Did you?"

Kier whipped his head up and locked his gaze with Danny's. "No. Never. Even though I sometimes had to feed, it never went any further. I never wanted anything more from any of them." He reached out and laid a hand on Danny's thigh. Warmth radiated through Danny's body from that point of contact.

"I was hurt to discover you'd lied to me about who you were all this time. Although I should have figured it out. I mean, we never left the house before sunset. That should have been my biggest clue."

"I'm so sorry. The last thing I ever wanted to do was hurt you. But I can't even begin to explain how scared I was to tell you the truth." Kier sucked in a breath. "Asking you out, knowing that you were a part of that group, was a huge risk. I was asking out someone who had issues with what I am. Talk about setting yourself up for a fall. But you were the hottest guy I'd ever seen, and it wasn't my brain running the show. The more time we spent together, the more amazing you became, the more I felt for you, and the more I worried. I didn't want to lose you, and I didn't want to lie. I was banking on what we felt for each other overriding your fear. So, I did nothing, said nothing. Then you found out like that and walked, no, ran all but screaming from me. I lost you and that absolutely gutted me, Dan."

Kier closed his eyes and turned his head away. Before he did Danny caught the flash of pain, and it stole his breath.

Danny's heart beat faster, and he bit his lip. He took a chance and reached out to cup Kier's cheek, bringing that brilliant arctic gaze back to his.

"I'm sorry too. In my head, I knew you were nothing like Kevin's attackers. But that night it was all too much. The fear was knee-jerk, but even more concerning to me was my reaction to seeing you feed."

Kier tried to shy away from his touch, but Danny wouldn't let him. He hopped off his stool and closed the distance between them. He cupped his hands around the back of Kier's neck.

"Yes, I was shocked. My brain was telling me that I should be disgusted, but I was also jealous and ridiculously turned on. I hated seeing your mouth on someone else. I wanted to be the one you were sucking on, giving you what you needed, and in that moment, I was appalled by my own thoughts. It's what kept me away for so long. I was coming to terms with everything I was feeling. I was putting the entire picture together in my head."

"And what did that picture look like?" Kier rested his hands on Danny's hips.

"It looked like I'd walked away from a great man because of my own fears, and because I clung to some preconceived, albeit justified, ideas that I didn't fully believe in anymore. Once I worked past the fear, then I had to address the jealousy. To be honest, I'm still not quite over that. I hate thinking about you with your hands and mouth on anyone else. I accept that it was necessary, but I'm not sure I'll ever be completely all right with you having that level of intimacy with someone else. When I started dreaming of you feeding from me, that's when I started working out a game plan to come back and convince you to try again."

Kier leaned forward and touched his forehead to Danny's. They stayed that way for a long moment. A weight lifted off Danny, and he couldn't help but smile.

"God, I missed this. I missed you." Danny wrapped his arms around Kier and hugged him close.

"Missed you too." Kier rested his head on Danny's shoulder.

"Can we do this? Can we wipe the slate clean and start over?"

Kier nodded and wrapped his arms around Danny, pulling their bodies flush. He lifted his head from Danny's shoulders, looked at Danny. He saw the slight furrow of Kier's brow and the hope in his eyes. He had a lot of work to do to repair the damage to their fragile relationship, but he'd do it. He'd put in the time, give Kier whatever he needed to trust in them again. He clasped Kier's head and pulled him down and into a kiss. Danny's head spun at first contact. The kiss stayed light, a reintroduction, but set off little sparks throughout out his body that had him buzzing from his lips to his toes. Their lips brushed, teeth nipped. He slid his hand down Kier's strong back, even as Kier slid his up and into his hair. He gasped at the slight sting as Kier fisted his fingers in his hair and gave a light tug. Kier sucked on his bottom lip, then slid the tip of his tongue along the inside. Their breath mingled and a soft moan escaped him. Kier sealed their mouths together again, and Danny reveled in the firm lips pressed to his. When the kiss ended, Danny clung to Kier, eyes closed, lips tingling, as he sucked in calming breaths until the blood racing through his system slowed. He eased his eyes open to find Kier smiling down at him. He smiled back, and for the first time in longer than he could remember, he thought just maybe everything would be all right.

# CHAPTER 8

MELISSA WOULD be pissed, but over the past few days, hell, the past few weeks, everything annoyed her. The fact that they hadn't found any trace of Danny Reynolds in twenty-four hours would just turn up the heat on her anger. Reynolds hadn't shown at his job; he hadn't gone back to his apartment. He'd dropped off the grid for the moment. What did she want Rogan to do? He couldn't work magic and conjure him up for her. Yes, he had a first name and a photo, but Rogan couldn't bring himself to turn those items over to her, or Lydecker for that matter.

While making Melissa wait for something she wanted made his life easier and more difficult, the status quo worked for him right now. Besides, figuring out how to get into Melissa's basement hideaway had moved above Danny Reynolds on Rogan's priority list. That's why he'd holed up in his office poring over copies of the Purity building blueprints. There had to be another way in, perhaps a fire corridor.

"Or there could be no way in at all because the damn room doesn't even exit." Rogan slapped his hands on his desk and blew out a hard breath. Either he'd found old building plans that predated the construction of that room, or the bitch had paid someone to alter the plans for her. He put his money on door number two. He wadded the paper and flung it across the room. It hit the wall with a soft, unsatisfying thump just as his phone began to vibrate on his desk. He glanced down at the screen and smiled for the first time all afternoon. Brian.

"Hey, Bri. What's up?" He leaned back in his chair and propped his feet on his desk.

"Are you coming home anytime soon?"

"I know I've been putting in some late nights, but I'm hoping to get out of here shortly. No promises, though."

A disbelieving grunt sounded over the phone. "Dude, you need to take a vacation. You're spending way too much time at that place."

"Well, if I didn't have to take care of my irritating little brother who insists on an education and eats like a starving wolverine, I might be able to take a few mental health days."

"Hey, I'm a growing boy."

"My ass. More like you have a tapeworm. Anyway, did you need something?"

"I just wanted to let you know I'm going to a party tonight with some friends."

"Where, when, and with who?" With Brian being nineteen and a sophomore in college, Rogan didn't expect that Brian would keep him up to date on his whereabouts at all times. Still, he appreciated when he did.

Brian huffed out a put-upon sigh. "I'll text you the deets so you don't have to freak out. But that's not why I called you."

"Cell phone stays on you at all times. Got it?"

"Yeah, yeah. You're such a mom sometimes." He'd gotten pretty good at filling the role ever since his and Brian's parents had been killed three years ago.

"Be safe. Don't do anything stupid, and I'll see you at home."

"You too. Don't work too hard. Those people aren't worth it."

"Hey. It's a good job. You know that. I may not agree with everything they do, but we need the money."

Unintelligible grumbles came over the phone.

"Call me if you need me."

"I will. Oh, and Mike?"

"Yeah?"

"I took another twenty bucks from the stash in your sock drawer. Dude, you really need a better hiding place."

"You little—" But the line went dead. Rogan chuckled. He sat watching the computer monitor cycle through the various camera feeds. When Melissa appeared on the feed, Rogan shoved up out of his chair. She stalked down the hall, a woman on a mission, and he knew exactly where she was going.

He retraced their route from the previous night, but this time he sped up as Melissa turned down the intersecting hallway. He peeked around the corner and watched her punch in a code on a lock pad. The locks disengaged with a soft click and she strode in. Rogan waited a beat after she disappeared through the door, then rushed to catch it before it slid shut.

He slipped in, pausing in the dim entry hall. It wound around, opening into another room. He didn't know what else Melissa kept in the room, but he couldn't see what lay around the corner. Moving any farther in would reveal his presence. He flattened himself against the wall and listened.

"A whole day. Another whole day and still nothing. How hard is it to catch one man? Seriously, if this is the best we've got, Purity is worse off than I thought." Machines beeped and hummed to life.

Rogan took a chance and inched a little closer to the end of the hall so he could get a better view. His eyes went wide at the sight of the state-of-the-art lab she'd assembled. She moved about the room flipping, switching, and pushing buttons until the low-level hum of hardworking equipment filled the room. Her back faced him, and he noticed that she kept looking toward the far end of the room, an area obscured by the hallway wall. When she started to turn around, he slid back into the shadows. How long had she had this setup in place? She'd stashed hundreds of thousands of dollars' worth of equipment down her for her own personal use on projects that, Rogan suspected, weren't sanctioned by the organization.

"You know, these blood results are fascinating. If—no, when— Lydecker gets his hands on this data, and believe me he will, there'll be no stopping him. I contemplated trying to destroy his samples, but considering how few people have access to his lab, that might bring too much attention my way. I'm not sure how much longer I can stomach playing the role of his dutiful little second-in-command." She snorted. "Best thing to do now is to just make sure he doesn't get his hands on a new lab rat. I'll be damned if I let him divert this agency any further from its true path." She spoke as though someone else listened to her, but she never received a response. Again,

Rogan risked discovery. He wanted a better look at the room. This time he spied her in front of a small white refrigerator. She pulled something out, but he couldn't see what. Then she walked slowly and steadily down to the hidden end of the room. Rogan itched to look around the other wall, but he couldn't take the risk. Instead he stuck his head farther in, looking into shadowed areas he couldn't get a good glimpse of before. *Damn hypocrite. She complains about Lydecker's experiments and here she is with her own secret lab that puts Lydecker's to shame, and yet she speaks of wasted resources.* He itched to get closer to do a thorough search of the room to figure out what she had going on in here.

"Dinnertime, Aiden."

Rogan froze. *Aiden?*

A soft plop followed her words. "Eat up. You've got to keep your strength up. And don't try and pull another one of those silly hunger strikes. You remember what happened last time." A soft growl sounded. Rogan's body went cold. *My God.* Did she have someone locked up down here? He swallowed hard and eased toward the wall that blocked his view of the rest of the space.

"Still a touchy subject, huh?" She laughed. "Don't let your dinner spoil to spite me. Oh, and try not to make a mess. Cleaning up after you is disgusting." Another louder growl filled the room. "I've got to run. I've got a specimen to catch, but I'll be back soon. I know how you miss me when I'm gone. Not to worry. You're going to have some company soon. Won't that be nice?"

Shit. Rogan moved back toward the entry door, hand on the handle as he strained to hear the sound of approaching footsteps. Nothing. He turned the handle, ready to move fast if he needed, but still no steps. A moment later the scrape of metal echoed through the room, followed by a soft thump.

Wait, seriously, did she have a secret exit from the building? He'd seen building blueprints and they held no record of an exit from this level. He waited. The silence stretched. He released the door handle and crept down the hallway. He blew out a breath and took a chance on looking around the blind corner. No Melissa, but he wasn't alone. His stomach churned. He needed to find out exactly who she held captive in this room. He drew in a deep breath and rounded the corner.

"Oh shit." Rogan stopped dead, sickness swirling in his stomach. The far end of Melissa's lab held a cage that contained a toilet, a sink, a narrow bed anchored to the wall, and a pale, gaunt, redheaded man. An iron shackle circled his ankle and kept him tethered.

The man shot a disinterested glance Rogan's way as he leaned forward and swiped the bag of blood off the floor and eyed it. "Do you know if this bag is drugged?"

"What?"

"Drugged. Did your boss put anything in this? One of the many ways the evil bitch likes to get her kicks is by slipping me something in my food. She knows I'll get hungry enough to eat it anyway."

Rogan's brain went numb. He couldn't process the sight in front of him, couldn't comprehend the horror of the story being told to him.

"I-I don't think so. I didn't see her add anything, but I can't say for sure. I'm guessing you're Aiden."

"Right in one, and you're one of her lapdogs." His emerald eyes met Rogan's.

"M-My name is Michael Rogan and I, uh, work for Purity, not her."

"Same difference." He shrugged. "What are you doing in here? I didn't think anyone but her could get in here."

"I could ask you the same."

"I'm enjoying these luxurious accommodations." Aiden gestured to his cage, then rolled his eyes.

"No. I mean how did you get here? How long have you been in here?"

"The how is simple. Melissa got really lucky. She caught me in a moment of weakness. I had a little too much to drink. Wandered out behind the bar. I don't know if she had the place under surveillance since it's a known vampire hangout or she got really damn lucky. All I remember is a sting in my neck and lights out. Next thing I know I come to in here. I've been here ever since, her personal test subject for the last month or two. I lost track of time."

"Isn't there anyone out there missing you? Friends? Family?"

Aiden snorted. "The witch got lucky with me. I've been known to be gone weeks at a time. I shut off my phone, leave my laptop home. I was just leaving on vacation when she grabbed me. My family likely hasn't even started missing me yet."

"Why?"

"I like to travel. You could say I've got itchy feet. Why is this relevant? I'm locked in an evil scientist's lab, and you want my life story? Seriously?"

Rogan rubbed his temple, trying to ease the beginnings of a headache. Enormous bills hung over his head, and working for Purity seemed like an easy way to pay them off. He didn't have to agree with them to work with them. He could ignore the stupidity and intolerance. Protect his community, yes. Create a cohesive unit from a group of men who were little more than a neighborhood watch run amok, no problem. But this.... He never signed on to break the law. He never agreed to be a party to kidnapping and torture.

"You know, this is the first full bag she's given me in a while. Some days she tosses me bags of blood so thin they could hardly count as sustenance. Bitch does it to keep me from reaching full strength. Keep the vampire weak and hungry, and he's yours do with as you please. At full strength, I might actually be able to rip the doors right off this wretched cage and run as fast and as far away from here as I could." He eyed the blood bag again. "I will be so annoyed if she's spiked it with something."

"Maybe you shouldn't drink that just in case." Guilt, horror, and anger all coiled through Rogan, leaving an oily sickness in their wake. "God, what the hell did I get myself into?"

"Bigotry gets a little harder to swallow after you've had a conversation with the thing you hate, doesn't it? Or does it make me one of the good vampires?" Aiden sneered at him.

"I don't hate you. I don't hate vampires."

"So why are you here?"

"I need the paycheck."

"You keep telling yourself that. There are other jobs out there."

"Look, they pay well, and I'm getting damn sick of having to justify my job decisions."

"Who asked you to?"

"You did. My brother, sort of." *Myself.* He'd never admit it out loud, but the more he saw and the deeper he got in this organization, the more he questioned and regretted the day he ever accepted the job.

"Ah, well. Maybe you should start rethinking your life choices. Let me tell you a little something about your boss."

"I've long suspected she's evil incarnate."

"Calling her evil is being kind. She's sick and sadistic. The last drug tests she ran on me erased my self-control and parts of my memory."

Rogan dropped his chin to his chest. "Don't tell me."

"What, you don't want to hear about the terrified screams that echoed through this lab and the scent of blood that drove me into a frenzy? I don't remember much of it, but I may have killed at least one person. She shoved some poor, defenseless bastard in here to see what I'd do. I drained him and left his body broken at my feet, either dead or unconscious." Aiden stepped back and slumped down on the bench anchored into the back wall of his cell. "I pray he was just unconscious."

Rogan stared at Aiden, a growing ache in his chest. No one should have to suffer through any of this torment. He couldn't walk away from this. Couldn't leave him here to keep suffering at Melissa's hands. Twisted bitch. How could anyone be so sadistic as to take pleasure in stealing someone's control and forcing them to do things they'd never willingly do, like some sort of private version of *The Hunger Games*? "I'm going to get you out of there." He started toward the wrought-iron prison.

"No. Stop." Aiden's command stopped him in his tracks. "She's got cameras in here. I know they're pointed at this end of the room. She likely has them everywhere, and they'll all be rigged for remote monitoring. Chances are she already knows you're in here with me. Who knows what she'll do once she realizes you've discovered her little secret."

Shit. He should have thought of that. If he tried to free this guy, Melissa would likely have them both on lockdown before he could blink. If, by some miracle, they got away, everyone he cared about would be in danger. Melissa would come after him hard and use every weakness she could exploit. Rogan balled his hands into fists. He'd be damned if she got anywhere near his family. She'd also never let her science experiment escape, couldn't risk him going to the press or the government.

A pained moan pulled him from his thoughts and back to Aiden. The already pale man went white and almost doubled over.

"What's wrong?"

"Hungry. Need to eat." He gestured with the bag of blood. "I guess I have to take my chances. You may want to get out of here just in case."

"I can't just leave you in here." Rogan looked around the room, at a total loss for what to do, how to help. When he looked back at Aiden, the man trembled from head to toe, and the look of sheer despair in his eyes stole Rogan's breath. "Drink, dammit. You're going to need all of your strength to escape this place."

He huffed out a laugh. "If you won't leave, then turn around while I do this."

"Nope."

Aiden cocked his head but kept his eyes locked with Rogan's as though daring him to keep looking as he did something that most members of Purity would find repellent. He lifted the bag, and his fangs lowered. He pierced the bag, then began to drink. The look on Aiden's face as he consumed the blood was that of a man getting his first drink of clean water after being lost at sea. He didn't guzzle; he savored despite the growling of his stomach. Rogan's gaze dipped to watch the motion of his pale throat as Aiden steadily swallowed. Despite his current state of dishevelment, something about Aiden struck Rogan in a way no one ever had before.

When Aiden had consumed every last drop, he crumpled the bag. As he licked away any stray droplets from his lips, Rogan followed the movement of his tongue. Rogan shifted his gaze to the floor as he took one breath.

"I have to give it to you, Rogan. I thought you'd flinch. Most of Purity would have been disgusted."

"I'm not like most of Purity."

"Not sure why, but I believe you." Aiden slid his gaze over Rogan in a slow, assessing once-over. "So now what?"

"Now I find a way to get you out of there."

"Not going to happen. These bars are solid iron. Melissa has the only key. You can't break me out of here, and Melissa probably already knows you've been in here with me. If we try anything, she'll have a platoon of soldiers on us before we get near the door."

Rogan nodded at the keypad on the wall. "What about her secret entrance over there?"

"Retina activated."

"Fuck." Rogan jammed his hands on his hips and dropped his chin to his chest as he racked his brain for an answer. "I can't just leave you here at her mercy."

"For now, we've got no choice. Any type of jailbreak would be a death sentence for both of us." Aiden paused.

Rogan stepped closer to the cell and dropped his voice to a whisper. Melissa had video in here, but he couldn't be sure about audio. "Is there anyone I can contact and let them know where you are?"

Aiden lowered his voice as well. "Alex Connelly and Kieran McCade. Kier owns a bar called the Haven. My sister Alex works there. It's at Third and Cherry, close to where the city divides."

"You mean at the edge of the predominately vampire section of town."

Aiden nodded.

"All right, I'm going." Rogan shoved his hands in his pockets. "Look, do your best to stay safe until I can get you out of here. I *will* get you out of here. I promise."

Aiden shook his head. "Don't make any promises you can't keep. But whatever you're thinking of doing, be quick about it. I'm pretty sure she's looking for her next victim to stick in this cage with me."

"Yeah, I know, but she's got to find him first. Keep fighting. Don't let her win." Rogan gave Aiden one last long look. Then, even though he hated to do it, he turned, walked out of the lab, and went in search of a vampire.

"KIER, I'M going to be in the stockroom. Alex sent me with a list of things she needs me to get to restock the front."

Kier stopped lowering chairs from the tabletops and smiled up at Danny. "I told you that you didn't have to do this if you didn't want to."

Danny smiled back. "I told you I'm enjoying myself." That little smile—hell, Danny's mere presence in his bar—tugged at something inside Kier, something he'd repressed for months. But after their talk earlier, he let joy and warmth spread through him.

"Kieran, if he's going to hang around all night, every night, he's going to make himself useful." They both turned their heads to find Alex watching them from behind the bar. She smiled and winked at Danny. "By the way, I just got a call from Tony. Fucker called out sick."

Kier and Alex started to laugh. Danny frowned. "What? I'm missing the joke."

"Dan, vampires don't get sick. Tony's probably holed up somewhere with the latest love of his life." Kier and Alex said the last few words in unison, then laughed again. This time Danny joined in.

Alex moved to the bar and snatched a rag from the countertop. She tossed it at Kier, who snagged it out of the air. "Give us a hand getting cleaned up and ready to open for the night. Even a man down we should still be staffed well enough to handle the crowd, but I'll let you know if I need help."

"Can do." Kier watched Danny disappear into the stockroom before turning back to his chores. Since their talk earlier, Danny seemed a little lighter, a little happier, and maybe more open to possibilities. Although the last might just be wishful thinking on Kier's part. And Kier couldn't stop thinking about that kiss.

Kissing Danny after all this time was like getting rescued after being lost adrift at sea. His taste was clean and sweet. The feel of him is his arms was indescribable. They fit together just right. Kier could so easily slip back into an old rhythm with him, but there was still too much uncertainty in Danny's situation and their relationship. Yes, their talk had gone a long way toward healing old wounds, but Kier couldn't shift gears that fast.

Alex flipped the switch to turn on the music. Kier jerked out of his thoughts as it blasted out of the mounted speakers circling the room.

"Sorry!" Alex adjusted the volume from blaring to tolerable.

"What are you doing, trying to make my ears bleed?"

She stuck her tongue out at him and started bouncing along to the rock song as she put away the items Danny had retrieved from the stockroom. Kier chuckled and continued to prep the bar. The song switched to some boy band pop, and Kier had to stifle a groan. Then he had to hold back a laugh when Danny whooped and started wiggling his slim hips and perfect ass to the beat as he pushed a dust mop across the floor. Kier licked his lips, watching Danny dance and shimmy his way around the room. When he shifted his gaze toward the bar, he found Alex staring at him. She raised an eyebrow, and his cheeks went warm.

When Danny started to sing off-key, Kier gave in and smiled like a fool.

"Jesus, Danny, you're going to shatter the windows with your screeching." Alex threw a towel at him.

Danny caught it and did a booty shake in her direction. "You're just jealous of my unusual talent."

"No, I'm jealous of your ears. I'm jealous of their ability to completely ignore how tone-deaf you really are."

Danny cackled and pretended to use the broom as a microphone. Kier wanted to cross to Danny, hold him in his arms, and kiss his awful singing into silence.

Kier shook his head. This was what life could be like, a man he cared about and good friends laughing and spending time together. He wanted that. God, he wanted it.

The pop song faded away as the opening strains of the all-too-familiar Ed Sheeran song rang out.

"Kier?"

He turned and looked into sparkling brown eyes that were filled with mutual memories of the first time they danced to this song.

Danny leaned the mop against the wall and held out a hand to Kier. "Dance with me."

He walked toward Kier, stopping an arm's length away. Kier stared at the steady hand reaching out to him. Even as he craved holding Danny in his arms, a small part of him wanted to hold back, to protect himself. Still, he reached out and let himself be drawn into the man, the music, and the memories. His gaze locked with Danny's as he tugged him close, holding him body to body. Danny slid his hands up Kier's chest and looped his arms around his neck. Kier rested his hands on Danny's hips. They started to sway, their movements fluid and familiar.

Kier closed his eyes and breathed deep. Danny's warm, clean aroma filled his senses. Nothing else in the world smelled as intoxicating as him. Nothing else could ignite a slow burn deep inside. Kier's breathing came a little faster, and his body went hard. He pressed his cheek to Danny's temple as he rubbed his hand up and down his back. Damn, he missed this.

"Do you remember the first time we danced to this?"

Kier nodded. "That country and western theme night you dragged me to. Thank God they broke up the blocks of country with other types of music."

"You had fun."

"I did after a few shots of bourbon."

Danny chuckled and gave him a light whack on the shoulder. "I remember you standing at the bar surrounded by a small harem of women. Man, were they disappointed when you walked over to me."

"Yeah, well, I was going into perfume overload."

"I was happy to be your escape route. Happy to be held in the arms of an amazingly beautiful man. Happy, period. You made me happy. You still do."

Kier leaned back so he could study Danny's eyes. He stopped dancing. He stood there continuing to hold the man who had the ability to destroy him in his arms. *What the hell am I doing?*

Danny reached up and caressed his cheek as he pressed even closer. Kier sucked in a breath as low-level currents of electricity thrummed through him. Danny carded his fingers through Kier's hair and set tingles dancing over his scalp. Danny started singing to him in that sexy, off-key manner about being taken into loving arms and kissed under the light of a thousand stars. He sang until their lips were a mere breath apart. Then the singing stopped, and Danny pulled Kier down and pressed a soft kiss to his lips as he slid his leg between Kier's. He brushed his thigh over the bulge in Kier's pants.

Danny tasted, nipping and nibbling and driving Kier out of his mind. The slow sampling didn't last long. This time Kier took the lead and claimed Danny's mouth. His familiar flavor flooded Kier's senses. He delved deep with his tongue, licking and caressing, as he took his time exploring the landscape of Danny's body with his hands.

Everything ceased to exist but this moment and this man. The fresh hunger hit Kier. He wanted to taste more than Danny's skin. He wanted to drink the rich blood that ran through his veins while he buried himself deep inside of Danny. Kier could hear the rapid thump of Danny's heart pounding, the rush of his blood.

*Mine*, he thought and growled as his fangs started to drop. His heart thundered; his breathing was loud and ragged. Only Danny could do this to him, make him forget everyone and turn into a ravenous beast.

The sharp call of Kier's name cut into his consciousness and allowed reality to creep in. When the call came a second time, he stepped back from Danny and sucked in a sharp breath. He opened his eyes to see a kiss-dazed Danny standing in front of him and Alex a few feet away, looking ready to tackle him should it be necessary.

"I'm fine, Alex. I promise." Guilt, need, and confusion all swamped him.

"Kier? What just happened?" Danny bit his lip and furrowed his brow as he reached out.

Kier stepped back. "I'm sorry. I got caught up in the moment, and things got a little out of hand."

"It's okay. If you need that from me, I'm offering willingly."

Kier took another step away. He needed to settle, to think, and he couldn't do it with Danny this close.

"Thank you. You don't know what that means to me to hear you say that, but taking that step is too much too soon. We need to talk to Sharon and figure out if your blood is safe to drink. We need to think before we take that step. We need to—I need to slow way down." Kier shoved a hand into his hair. "I need some air."

He started to walk past Danny, but instead he paused and brushed the back of his finger over Danny's cheek. "I'll be back in a bit." With that said, he turned and strode off down the hallway to his office, leaving a stunned Danny in his wake.

# CHAPTER 9

"HEY, BRI." Rogan spoke into a Bluetooth earpiece as he drove away from the Purity compound.

"Hey! Where the hell have you been? Did you even come home last night?"

"In late, out early. What can I say?"

"You work too hard for those people."

"We've already talked about this, Bri." Rogan blew out a breath.

"Yeah, yeah, money, blah." His brother's snort of disgust sounded through the phone.

"Look, I need you to do something for me. I need you to be extra vigilant when you leave the house."

"What, why?"

"Because there's some bad stuff going down on the job, and I don't want you to get caught up in any of it. So just watch your back."

"Of course." A long silence fell between the two men. "Mike, whatever's happening, it's dangerous, isn't it? Don't answer that. I already know."

Rogan shoved his hand through his hair. Fucking Purity and Melissa Moran. He resented that they'd put him in this position. He never wanted to worry his brother, and now he could hear it in every word he spoke.

"Just quit, Mike. Walk away. We don't need their blood money. You don't even believe in their fucking cause. I'll get a job and help out with the bills. We'll be fine."

Rogan clenched his fist on the steering wheel. "I don't want you to have to do that."

"I won't be the first college student on the planet to also have a job. But I'd much rather get a job or drop out of school altogether than have you risk your life for these crazy Purity people, or worse, have them coming after you."

"You will not quit school. We will figure something out, but for now I need you to be careful while I take care of this one last thing. I've stumbled across something I can't just walk away from."

"Do me a favor. Don't be a hero."

"I'll do my level best not to."

Brian barked out a laugh. Rogan pulled his SUV up to the curb outside of the Haven bar and killed the engine. "I need to go. I'll come home as soon as I'm done here."

"Please, be careful. You're all the family I have left."

"I will. I love you, Bri."

"I love you too, Mike."

Rogan disconnected the call, then sat and watched the bar for a few minutes. A steady stream of people came, but no Purity patrols came by. Hopefully he'd be able to blend in, find the people he needed to talk to, and then get back out unnoticed. He drew in a breath and climbed out. After crossing the street, he slipped into the bar. Blaring music and the voices of all the patrons created a dull roar. He scanned the large space filled with people dancing and drinking. In the back, he saw people shooting pool, throwing darts, and playing pinball. He went still and blinked twice when he saw Danny Reynolds wandering through the crowd. "I'll be damned," he murmured.

Rogan stepped up to the bar and signaled the bartender, an attractive woman with milk-pale skin and a long red braid running down her back.

"Hey, there. What can I get you?" She smiled and set a cocktail napkin in front of him.

"I'll take whatever you have on tap and a little information."

She leaned in and smiled at him. "What is it you want to know?"

"I'm hoping you can point me in the direction of Kieran McCade."

Her smile dropped, and she gave him a slow, suspicious once-over. "Why are you looking for Kier?"

"I have a message for him."

"From who?"

"Look, since you're giving me the third degree, I'm assuming he's around somewhere. I'd just like to talk to him. It's a life or death matter."

She narrowed her eyes at him, then pulled her phone out of her pants pocket. "Give me a second." She fired off a message, then turned to help another patron.

When she finished, she checked her phone, looked up at him, and then said, "Come with me." She made her way out from behind the bar, calling out to the other bartender as she went. "Tom, I'm stepping out. Keep an eye on things for me. Pull someone from the floor if you need help." The other bartender waved at her, then went back to chatting with a blonde in a tight black dress. Rogan followed the redhead down a dark hallway and was shown into an office. As he walked in, he goggled at the luxurious space hidden away in the back of a bar.

"Who are you and what do you want?"

Rogan turned his attention to the muscular man behind the wide wooden desk. "I'm assuming you're Kieran McCade."

The man leaned back in his chair and crossed his arms. The redheaded bartender still lingered in the door, giving him a narrow-eyed glare.

"I'm Michael Rogan. I'm here with a message from Aiden."

"Aiden." The redhead stepped closer. "Is he all right?"

"No, he's not. For the last month, he's been held captive inside the Purity compound." The woman gasped. Kieran McCade's expression went from concerned frown to thundercloud angry.

"You know this how?"

Rogan blew out a breath and braced himself as he looked Kieran straight in the eye. "Because I work for Purity, and I found Aiden locked up in a cell in the sub-basement. He sent me to you."

"You what? No!" The explosion came, but not from who he expected. The redhead had him up against the wall with her arm across his windpipe before he even realized she'd moved. A deep red glow shone from the depths of her eyes. "How dare you come here, you Purity bastard. How could you see a man locked up and just leave him? Aiden is a kind soul. He'd never hurt a fly. You can't tell me he warranted imprisonment."

"I didn't say he was in—" Rogan choked out the words, then tapped at her arm when he couldn't pull in enough air to finish his sentence.

"Alex, let the man breathe. We won't get any information about Aiden if you kill him now."

When Alex released him, he bent over, bracing his hands on his knees and sucking in air.

"Talk. Now."

"He's not in a detention cell. He's locked away in a private lab, and I left him there because I couldn't get him out, but I'm hoping you can. He's being kept weak so that he can't break his ankle chain or break the door off the hinges."

"How the hell was he captured in the first place?"

"Likely some form of a tranquilizer. Purity has an extensive antivampire R&D department, and they're always coming up with nasty little inventions to tranq, maim, or kill a vampire."

Kieran came to stand directly in front of him, forcing Rogan to look up slightly. "Why is Purity coming to me and sharing its secrets? How do I know this isn't some kind of a setup?"

"Because if I were setting you up, then I wouldn't voluntarily tell you that you might want to keep a better eye on Daniel Reynolds. Do you know him? I just saw him out in the main room. The director and assistant director of Purity both want to get their hands on him bad."

Again, Rogan found himself pinned to the wall, this time with Kieran's hand around his throat. Rogan's own hands were thrown up in surrender. Kieran shot a look at Alex. "Dammit, I knew those were Purity soldiers the other night. Go get him. Now." She nodded and slid out of the office.

When Kieran turned back to Rogan, he got in Rogan's face and all but growled. Rogan's heart hammered. His breath rushed in and out of him. He thought feeding time in the tiger habitat at the zoo would be less intimidating than facing this man alone.

"Look, man, I'm not here to hurt anyone. I'm certainly not here on Purity's behalf. I'm here to try and stop something terrible from happening. I was ordered to do whatever it takes to apprehend him. While I may have been willing to overlook certain aspects of

Purity's ideology, I'm not willing to stoop to kidnapping. I'm damn well not willing to stand by and knowingly let an innocent soul be tortured and tormented. I hated leaving Aiden in that cage, but I can't get him out without help. So, here I am giving up my livelihood and compromising my brother's education and possibly the roof over his head." He tugged on Kieran's wrist. "Please?" He tried to keep his tone calm and even.

Kieran released him and stepped back. "What does Purity want with Danny, and how the hell did you find us?"

"Like I said, Aiden. And, by the way, if he hadn't directed me to find you, I wouldn't have had a clue that Danny was hiding out here. As to what they want from him, they want his blood."

"So, they know about the anomalies in his blood?"

"Yeah. They analyzed a blood sample we took from his apartment and from the scene of his altercation behind the library. Now the top two researchers want to get their hands on him for very different reasons."

"Why? What do you know about his condition?" Kieran continued to frown at him.

"Me? Nothing. I'm not a scientist, but I can tell you this. Lydecker wants him because Danny killed his whackjob vampire son. Both he and Melissa want him because the changes in his blood are extremely unique. Again, I don't quite understand the science, but suffice it to say, they think his blood holds the key to helping them develop a cure."

"A cure for what?"

Rogan just stared at him and saw the moment understanding dawned on Kieran's face.

"Shit!"

"That about sums it up. When Danny got attacked by and exchanged blood with Jared, something about his makeup changed, and because of this, he's brought down one big fucking boatload of trouble on himself."

"I don't understand. Jared attacked Danny. Danny was defending himself. How can they blame him for that?" Kieran paced away and shoved his fingers through his hair.

"Look, what you need to understand is that Jared was not all that mentally stable when he was fully human. When he went through the change, it unleashed the inner sociopath that he'd just barely managed to keep in check. The other thing that Jared's change did was set Lydecker on the mission to cure vampirism."

"So, what does that have to do with me?"

Rogan looked toward the door to find a wide-eyed Danny Reynolds standing there with hands clenched at his sides.

"When you killed Jared, you not only killed Lydecker's son, you destroyed his own personal lab rat."

Danny blinked, opened his mouth to speak, and then blinked again. "You're telling me this sick fuck experimented on his own child? Why? How could he do something like that?"

Kieran crossed to Danny and slid an arm around his waist. Danny leaned in, giving some of his weight to Kieran.

"Look, ever since his son was 'infected,' Lydecker has been searching for a way to cure him. He was using every resource he had available to him at Purity to research and experiment. A small part of me feels bad for the man. At the core, he was a father trying to save his son, no matter how flawed. Now he's a grieving father and he's taking all of that and dumping it into his work, which has come to a frustrating halt for him. On one hand he wants Danny to pay for taking his son's life, but on the other, he wants access to his blood and the secrets that it holds."

"Which motivation is stronger for Lydecker, revenge or science?" Kieran asked.

"To Lydecker's way of thinking, Jared gave his life to the cause. But now that he's found another similar specimen, he can continue to look for a cure for the vampiric affliction in Jared's honor." Rogan rolled his eyes but then paused. He studied the two men as they took in his words. Danny pressed closer, almost burrowing into Kieran's side and reaching out to interlace his fingers with Kieran's.

"Honestly, though, Lydecker is the lesser of your concerns. If Melissa gets her hands on him…. Let's just say nothing good will come of it. Lydecker will keep Danny alive because he needs him. With Melissa…."

"Melissa? Who's that?" Danny shifted scared eyes from Rogan to Kieran.

"She's number two in Purity's food chain, just behind Lydecker. She works in the lab with him but is also heavily involved in the security side of things. It's enabled her to grab hold of way too much power. Her vision for Purity is very different from Lydecker's, and she'll do whatever it takes to make sure things run her way. Her master plan doesn't include finding a cure. She wants all vampires wiped off the planet. If she gets her hands on Danny, he won't last very long at all, especially since his blood might be the key Lydecker needs to find the cure."

"So, what are you suggesting we do?" Danny's voice cracked on the last word. Kieran eased him over then down onto the plush love seat.

"That, I guess, is up to you. But I would think getting Aiden out of the Purity compound would be the first thing on the agenda."

"We're absolutely getting Aiden out of there." Alex marched back into the office. "Kier, I'll be damned if I let these Purity bastards kill my brother."

*Brother!* A small knot in Rogan's gut released. Hell, he hadn't even realized that this woman's connection to Aiden had been bothering him until right that second. The fact that he'd been worried at all was ridiculous. He'd met the man once and under less than ideal circumstances. Anything beyond soothing a troubled conscience shouldn't even be a thought in his head.

"Why would you help us?" Kieran's question snatched Rogan out of his thoughts. Rogan looked at Kieran.

"Suffice it to say I've hit my threshold for blind acceptance. When you don't see most of the bad that's going on, it's easy to put it out of your mind and work the job. I mean, I have a family to take care of and I'm doing the best I can, but this—" Rogan shook his head. "Seeing Aiden in that cage, hearing his story, it made all the horrible real. I couldn't just stand by anymore."

The room fell silent for a long moment. Then Kieran nodded.

"I also couldn't stand by and watch an innocent victim be hunted down to be a guinea pig for, to borrow your phrase, those Purity bastards."

Alex snorted out a laugh, and a small smile settled on her lips for a second.

"Trust me. Both Melissa and Lydecker want Danny found at all costs. You can get out of town, but I don't know if it will matter. They will put everything they've got into finding Danny."

"Fuck. Fuck, fuck, fuck." Danny braced his elbows on his knees and covered his face with his hands.

Kieran claimed the seat next to Danny and rubbed slow circles over his back. "We will figure this out. I'm not going to let anything happen to you."

Rogan studied the two men. He couldn't think of anything he wouldn't do to help someone he cared about if they landed in this kind of trouble. And the image of Aiden flickered in and out of his mind.

Kieran looked at Rogan and cocked his head. "Tell me something. How close are they to finding an actual cure?"

Rogan frowned, then shrugged. "I'm not sure. Like I said, I'm not a scientist."

"Is there any way we can get our hands on a copy of their notes?"

Danny gasped and whipped his gaze up. Their gazes locked with laser intensity.

Kieran clasped Danny's hands. "I'm thinking if we're going to go in after Aiden, maybe we can find something to help you out too."

Rogan scratched his head. "That could prove to be a little more challenging, but let's see what we can do. Let me go into headquarters tomorrow and see what I can find out about where the information is kept. I can also bring you copies of the building plans, although I've recently learned they aren't 100 percent accurate. I'll add the missing parts that I know about, but there may be more structural differences. Still, they should be complete enough to use to mount any type of a rescue operation. Wait to hear from me. I'll be in touch soon."


MELISSA MORAN slipped through the door to the Haven and had to suppress the urge to sneer in disgust. Vampires littered the room like an enormous intrusion of cockroaches that needed to be exterminated. She slid through the room toward a corner table that gave her a clear view of most of the space. She sat with her back to the wall, watching and waiting.

She'd known that Rogan was in her lab almost from the moment he'd slipped through the door. She had cameras everywhere. But she let it go, let him in on a part of her little secret to see what he would do with the information. And what did he do? He came straight here, to a cesspool of vampires.

She'd be doing the world a favor if she struck a match and turned this place into a blazing inferno. She'd be a hero to rid the world of these ravening beasts who forced innocent people to join their ranks. Who turned good men into murderers. Who destroyed lives and families. Rage, white and blinding, threatened to consume her.

"Excuse me, ma'am, can I take your order?"

Melissa whipped her head up and gave the waitress a look that had her backing up a step.

She blinked, cleared her mind, and reset her expression. She ordered a glass of water for the sake of blending. When the girl scrambled away, Melissa took a few minutes to calm herself. Losing control would solve nothing. The waitress returned a minute later, deposited a glass on the table in front of her, and scurried off again. Melissa glanced down at the glass, then looked away. She didn't deign to touch it.

Thirty minutes later she started to think she went to the wrong location. She'd assumed Rogan had gone into the bar because he'd parked his car directly across the street, but she'd only managed to put a tracker on the man's car, not the man himself. She stood to leave, then froze. Her brows shot up as Rogan emerged from a dimly lit hallway. He made his way through the bar, heading straight for the exit. She dropped back down into the chair, trying to make herself inconspicuous, and watched him leave. She didn't attempt to follow him. She and Rogan needed to have a little chat, but not right now, not until she knew the true depths of his betrayal.

Melissa ground her teeth and pushed up from her seat again. She needed to get out of this place, away from these "people." As she started for the door, shattering glass snagged her attention. She looked over to see Daniel Reynolds walking toward a distraught woman standing over a pile of beer mug shards. She stopped dead, rage erupting through her like a flash fire. Days. Purity had spent days searching for Reynolds, and here he stood in the same location that her head of security had just left.

Melissa pulled out her cell phone and dialed. "I need the shift commander in my office in an hour. I've located our mark. We need to figure out how we're going to bring him in."

"ALEX. LEAVE it. Leave the glass. I've got this." Danny crouched next to Alex, who collected the large broken pieces of the beer mugs with trembling hands.

"It's fine," Alex said. "I broke them, I can clean them up." Danny wanted to help, wanted to help alleviate some of her fear, anger, and worry, but she'd refuse. In this room full of people, Alex would not appreciate anything that tarnished her tough-woman reputation even a little.

He looked up at Kier, who moved to stand next to Alex. Kier put his hands on her shoulders and coaxed her to her feet. Then he led Alex out of the busy bar and into his office.

Danny gave them a few minutes alone while he helped with the removal of the remaining broken glass. When he finished, he returned to Kier's office and stopped in the doorway but didn't enter the room. He didn't want to intrude on this moment between two longtime friends.

Alex paced the office, hands clenching then releasing over and over, her eyes flashing a brilliant red. Kier leaned against the front edge of his desk watching her, waiting. After five laps across the room, she broke.

"They have him, Kier. For a month those bastards have had my brother doing God knows what to him. I don't—" She shook her head and swallowed. "How could I have not known? I've been going about my merry way and I never once thought to check on him. Not once."

Kier reached out and took her hand. "Alex, he was on vacation, or so we thought. You had no reason to think differently. No reason to call. To check up on him. It's just his way to disappear every so often. You know that."

She leaned in and rested her head on his shoulder. "I know. It just kills me to think of him scared and hurt and—"

An ache formed in Danny's chest at the pain and worry in Alex's voice. He couldn't imagine how terrifying this must be for her. He didn't know what he'd do if it were Kier who'd been taken and tortured. He suspected Alex held up better than he would.

Kier pulled her into a hug. "Then don't think about what's been done to him. We can't change it, but we can stop it. Let's just focus on getting him out."

"How? How are we going to get into the Purity compound and get him out? That building is practically a fortress."

"I think Rogan may be our best option. Any type of obvious attack on the Purity facility would either get us killed, spark a war between vampires and humans, or both."

She paced away from Kier. She sat on the edge of the couch with her elbows braced on her knees and her head propped in her hands. "Do you think we can trust this Rogan guy? I mean, he works for the enemy."

"I don't think we have much choice in the matter."

"I hate that," Alex grumbled. "What if this is a setup? What if it's just an elaborate plan to get their hands on Danny? It's stupid to take on a bar full of vampires. But a squad full of Purity soldiers could subdue a couple of vampires who stride onto their turf like lambs to the slaughter."

Kier scratched his chin. "I think Rogan is smart enough to realize I would never bring Danny with me into Purity's facility."

"That's what I mean. He locks you up or worse kills you, and Danny is left unprotected. It's a hell of a lot easier to take him without you around, Kier." Danny's lungs stopped working for a long moment. The thought of anyone hurting Kier to get to him stole his breath, made him sick to his stomach. He must have made a sound because both Kier and Alex looked over at him.

Kier held out a hand, and Danny crossed to him. Kier wrapped an arm around his shoulders, and Danny wrapped his arm around Kier's waist and settled into the curve of his body, relishing the warmth and contact.

Alex held out a hand and Danny clasped it. "So what's the plan?" Danny asked.

Kier brushed his lips against Danny's temple and then said, "I think the best thing we can do is wait to hear from Rogan."

"You really think this Rogan guy is playing straight with us?" Alex cocked her head at Kier. "We're just supposed to take him at his word that he's with Purity. Hell, he could be setting us up for anything."

Kier shrugged. "I suppose anything is possible, but walking into a vampire bar and giving your adversary inside information doesn't seem to be the best plan of action. I think the best thing we can do is wait to hear from Rogan. I could be wrong, but I didn't sense any reason to distrust his story. Still, just like always, we watch our backs."

Alex frowned but nodded. "I just hate waiting. I want Aiden out of there now." She scrubbed her hand down her face and flopped back on the couch.

"I know you do, but we need to be smart about this." Kier laid a hand on Alex's arm. "Now do me a favor and go home. You need to clear your head, get away from people for the evening. I can take care of the bar tonight."

Alex shook her head. "No. I need the distraction of work. I promise, no more broken glass tonight."

"Are you sure?" Kier asked.

She smiled and nodded as she rose. She crossed to Kier and clasped his shoulder. Their eyes met and some sort of silent communication passed between them. Then she turned and headed out of the room. When she reached the door, she glanced back over her shoulder at Kier. "Hey. Do you need me?" Alex tapped her neck.

Kier shook his head. "I'm good for now."

Alex raised an eyebrow at him. "Promise me you'll see to that issue from earlier."

Kier's face went blank. His eyes shifted to Danny, then back to Alex. "I've already made arrangements to do that."

"Good," she said, then disappeared from the room.

Danny shifted to stand in front of Kier. He ran his hands up and down Kier's arms. "Are you doing all right? It can't have been easy learning about your friend."

Kier rested his hands on Danny's hips and tugged him close. "I'm fine. Worried about Aiden, but at least he's still alive. How about you? It's good news if Purity really does have a cure in the offing. We may be able to fix you after all."

Danny stared into Kier's eyes, but he couldn't read him. Once again Kier had locked himself behind those shields he so expertly constructed. "I honestly don't know how I feel. It's a lot to take in and still a big maybe. While they may be working toward a cure, they don't have it yet."

Kier dropped his hands to his sides, started to move away, but Danny wrapped his arms around his neck, refusing to let go. "Listen to me. If this cure becomes a reality, I'll have some decisions to make. But, even if I decide I want to find a way to remain human, that doesn't mean I'm going to run screaming from you again. If I opt to remain human, for now, that doesn't mean I'm rejecting who and what you are. No, I'm still not sure if I can ever see myself as a vampire, but give me time, Kier. Give me a chance to figure it all out."

Danny leaned in and pressed a soft kiss on Kier's lips. He closed his eyes and breathed in the warm, earthy scent of Kier. When he opened his eyes, he cupped Kier's face so he couldn't look away. "Whatever the future brings, whatever questions or doubts I may have, I want to figure it all out with you, if you'll let me."

Kier rested his forehead against Danny's. "I think I can do that."

"Good. First question. What did Alex mean? What issue does she want you to address?"

# CHAPTER 10

A BITTER, cold breeze blew, penetrating Danny's coat, making him shiver. He crowded close to Kier while Kier fished in his pocket for the house keys.

"Hurry up, K. I'm about to turn into an icicle."

Kier snorted. "You need a warmer coat if you're that cold after walking one block."

"You need to pick up the pace. This wind is killing me." He huddled closer to Kier, using his bulk to block the frigid gusts. They barreled through the door when it opened, and Danny headed for the back stairs leading downstairs. As he approached the stairway, he noticed a light go on in his peripheral vision. He turned to see Kier entering the parlor on the main floor. Danny backtracked and stuck his head in through the entrance.

"Hey. What's going on? Aren't you coming down?"

Kier glanced at him, down at his watch, then back at the door. "Go ahead to bed. I'll be down in a few minutes."

Danny frowned and strode into the room. He stopped in front of Kier and cocked his head. "What's going on?"

Kier looked back at the door. "Nothing. I just need to take care of something. Go on to bed. It's been an eventful evening."

Danny shook his head. "I'm not going anywhere until you tell me what's going on with you."

Kier shoved a hand through his hair. "I have a… dinner date. So to speak."

Danny frowned. "A dinner date?" Then the light bulb went on. "Oh! A dinner date. You're going to…."

"Yes, Danny. I'm going to feed. I'm going to drink someone's blood. So why don't you head on down before Gina gets here."

Danny shook his head. "Not going to happen. I need to see this. Need to be a part of this. I need to see how it works." Danny stepped up to Kier and raised a hand to cup his face. "I want to experience this with you."

Kier closed his eyes and pulled Danny close. Danny slid his hand up Kier's firm muscled back as Kier rested his forehead against his. "I'm not sure this is a good idea. I don't know that you're ready to see this yet."

"If everyone waited until they were truly ready to do something, very little would ever get accomplished." A thought that had poked at him all night forced its way into his mind. His mouth dropped open as realization dawned. "This is the issue Alex wanted you to attend to, isn't it? When we were dancing earlier, you wanted to bite me, drink from me. Didn't you?"

"Yes. Like I said, I got caught up and the hunger got the better of me."

"Hunger? But you've been, um, eating."

"Cold feeds. Every so often a vampire needs warm, fresh blood. If we go too long, the craving becomes a compulsion. It's what causes random vampire attacks to happen sometimes." Kier shifted his gaze away. "I've gone a little too long since my last—" Kier cleared his throat. "Warm feed. If Alex hadn't snapped me out of it, I might have gone too far."

Danny wrapped his arms around Kier, stared into his eyes. "Never happen."

The doorbell rang, interrupting their moment. Danny pressed a short fast kiss to Kier's lips. The contact sent a quick spark of electricity shooting through him. "Go answer the door." Danny released him and stepped back. Kier searched Danny's eyes for one long moment, then nodded and went to let in their guest.

"Hey, Kier," a woman purred as she walked into the house. "It's been a while. I was glad to hear from you." She ran a hand down Kier's arm as she strode past and into the parlor.

Danny clenched his teeth, resisting the urge to tell her to keep her hands to herself. She paused for a moment when she spotted him, then upped the seductive wattage of her smile and swaggered toward him. "You didn't tell me this was going to be a ménage, Kier. Name's Gina."

"Danny."

Her eyes went wide, and she shot a sly smile at Kier. "So, this is the famous Danny. You didn't tell me he was so good-looking. This is going to be fun."

Danny cocked an eyebrow at Kier. He'd talked about Danny to other people. Interesting.

"It's just me tonight, Gina. He's just going to watch."

She smirked. "I can work with that."

Kier actually blushed. "Knock it off." She chuckled low and seductively. She shed her leather coat and tossed it over the back of a chair.

She met Danny's gaze and held it as she walked to Kier, plastered her back to his chest, reached up, hooked a hand around the back of his head, and tugged him toward her neck. Kier's fangs extended as he lowered his mouth to her smooth throat. He hesitated, flicking his gaze to Danny, then away. Then he closed his eyes and sank in his teeth. She gasped and clutched at him when he sucked on her neck. Gina moaned, a sound of pure ecstasy.

Danny shoved his hands into his pockets and locked his knees. It took everything in him not to march over to the woman and yank her away from his man. He wanted Kier's hands on him. Wanted Kier's mouth on his skin, drinking from him. His entire body went hot and hard. His breathing picked up speed.

Gina's gasps and moans got louder as she writhed against Kier. Danny couldn't take much more of this. He needed to touch Kier. Needed Kier's hands on him. Needed Gina gone. Just as his patience broke, Kier pulled his mouth away from her neck. Danny blew out a hard, steadying breath, but his body still throbbed.

"Damn you, Kier. I just needed another minute more."

Kier smiled at the pouting woman. "Maybe next time, Gina."

"You big tease. Anytime you need me, just call. Anytime." She leaned up and kissed his cheek.

Kier laid a hand on her arm. "Are you okay to get home?"

"I'll be fine. I've got a ride waiting outside for me," she said as she reached for her coat. She flashed one last satisfied smile, then strutted toward the door. The front door closed with a soft click.

Kier's dark gaze met Danny's. Held it. "Not as bad as you expected it to be?"

Danny shook his head in response. He crossed to Kier, reached up to take his face between his hands. "It was the hottest thing I've ever seen." He claimed Kier's mouth, pouring every ounce of emotion swirling inside him into that kiss until his lungs screamed for air. He released Kier's lips and sucked in a long, slow breath. "Next time you feed, you feed from me. Are we clear?"

Kier froze in place. "Are you sure? Drinking your blood doesn't freak you out?"

Danny nodded and slid his hand down Kier's chest. He paused to flick his nipple through his T-shirt, then gripped handfuls of his shirt. "I'm sure. And, while I know it's probably unrealistic, I don't want your mouth on anyone but me. I don't want you sharing something that intimate with anyone but me." He tugged Kier's shirt up and off.

Kier growled at him and pulled their bodies flush.

"Last question. Is this safe? Will my blood hurt you?"

"It shouldn't. Can't make me any more of a vampire then I already am, but let's get the all clear from Sharon first. Better to be sure. After that, every part of you is mine."

Danny chuckled at that, then closed his eyes and reveled in the press of body to body. He breathed in Kier's unique, rich, spicy scent. *God, the man smells good.* He pressed his nose to the junction of Kier's neck and shoulder for a long moment. Then he turned his head to run the tip of his tongue along the long, lean muscle. He tasted the faintest hint of salt. As he licked the flavor from his lips, he lifted his gaze and got trapped by the bluest eyes he'd ever seen. Neither of them spoke. Words would only break whatever spell had woven itself around them. Danny wasn't taking that chance. He planned to enjoy every second of this.

In that moment, the rest of the world floated away. Nothing important existed except him, Kier, and this moment. Keeping their gazes locked, Danny slowly moved up Kier's body until their lips all but touched. He ran the tip of his tongue along the crease of Kier's lips. He cupped his hand around Kier's neck, pulling him to him, closing the remaining space between them. For a moment, Kier stood still, not participating but not resisting, and then his lips parted, giving Danny access to the warm interior of his mouth. Their tongues tangled, sipping and sampling until air became a necessity. Danny caressed his way down Kier's body, and his mouth and tongue followed, leaving a hot wet trail as he made his way to the tightened nub of Kier's nipple. He sucked hard, saw Kier's hands clench, heard Kier cry out his name in the low raspy tone that was so familiar, and Danny knew he had him. He'd heard that tone countless times in the past, and he reveled in the fact that he could still pull it out of Kier. Kier wrapped his hand in Danny's hair, and his body arched up.

"Damn, Danny."

Danny smiled, pressing a kiss to his chest. He dropped to his knees, unzipped Kier's jeans, and tugged them down to reveal the treasure inside. He nuzzled Kier's abs and the crease of his thigh before pressing his face into the patch of hair at his groin. He breathed in the musky scent of Kier, steeping himself in aroma and sensation. Kier's fingers slid through his hair, over his shoulders, his back, touching everything that he could reach. Demanding more.

Danny moved lower, trailing hot breath over the long length of Kier, close enough to taste, touch, but teasing them both. He lapped at the tip, a long, wet taste. Kier widened his stance, then clutched Danny's hair. Danny loved Kier's responses to his touch. Loved that he could drive him wild with pleasure. He rewarded them both by taking Kier in his mouth. He sucked the tip, swirling his tongue around the head. He gripped the base of Kier's cock, working him with both mouth and hands. The sounds coming from Kier sent heat rushing through Danny.

"Christ. More. Need you."

Danny smiled around that lovely erection, then went back to rocking Kier's world. He reached to massage the heavy sac between his Kier's legs. Took Kier in deeper, running his tongue along the thick vein that coursed down the length of his shaft. He reached for his own cock, freed it from the confines of his jeans, and stroked himself. Heat and need raced through him, ratcheting his desire up to the next level.

Kier moaned, easing back from Danny. Kier pulled him to his feet and, with preternatural speed, had Danny undressed and pinned to the floor.

Danny laughed as he met Kier's sexy smile. "Would it be corny to say you sure know how to sweep a guy off his feet?"

"Extremely." Danny shivered as Kier's warm breath and the low rumbled word caressed his ear. Kier claimed his mouth, running his tongue along the crease, coaxing his lips to part again. He began to explore Danny's body, trailing his fingers down his sides, gripping his hips, and pulling them tight against each other. Danny moaned, doing some exploring of his own as he sucked Kier's lower lip. He'd never been able to get enough of Kier's flavor when they'd been dating, and nothing had changed during the time they'd been apart. The man could take him from zero to scorching in seconds. Danny released his mouth, then buried his face in the curve of Kier's neck, breathing in his scent before nipping and sucking on his skin, skimming along his jawline, stopping to feast on his earlobe. He lost himself to the magic Kier's hands could weave.

Kier skimmed his hands over Danny's hips down the back of his thighs. They ground against each other, creating a delicious friction, but he didn't want to go over this way. He wanted Kier in him in every way, driving him out of his mind with pleasure.

"Want you. Need to feel you, taste you." Danny's heart thundered, and ragged breaths sawed out of his lungs.

"I'm right here. I'll take care of you."

"We need—"

"I know. Be right back." Danny's body didn't even have time to get cool from the loss of body heat before Kier's returned. He wrapped arms and legs around Kier as he offered a kiss. Kier accepted, devouring him with breath-stealing kisses. Their tongues twined and explored. Danny's body throbbed. He clutched Kier to him as though he might disappear, and he ate at his mouth as though the intoxicating flavor would be the last thing he'd ever taste. Danny arched when a slick finger tickled the sensitive, puckered flesh of his rear entrance, gently pressing against it until Kier could ease a finger inside him.

Danny cried out as his breath backed up in his throat. He squirmed, wanting more of that finger inside him, reveling in the tiny sparks that danced through him. Kier's finger moved slowly but steadily, in and out, letting Danny adjust to the intimate invasion. When the ring of muscle loosened, he inserted a second finger, pushing in farther, searching for and finding that sweet spot that sent electricity zinging through Danny. He cried out, "Oh shit! Do that again, damn."

"Liked that, did you?"

Danny heard the smirk in Kier's voice. The one that said he knew exactly what he'd done to Danny and it would keep getting better. Danny all but purred, then cried out when the amazing sensations stopped.

By the time Kier deemed him ready, he had him moaning, writhing, and this close to going off like a geyser.

"Fuck me, Kier. Now! Right fucking now."

"I'm all yours, love." Kier panted; the warm puffs of air wafted over Danny's wet lips just before he kissed him hard. He placed his cock against Danny's waiting entrance, then pressed forward, easing his way in. Kier waited a few moments to give Danny time to adjust. Danny clawed at him, needing the solid, grounding presence of Kier's body under his hands.

"Move, Kier. Please, do something, anything. I'm going crazy."

Kier set a hard driving pace designed to blow Danny's mind.

"Yeah…. Oh yeah…," Danny chanted as Kier fucked him to the verge of oblivion.

"Shit…. Kier… gonna…."

"Gonna come?"

"Yeah, yeah, God, yeah."

Kier nipped Danny's earlobe, then licked his neck over the pulse point before murmuring, "Next time." He latched on to Danny's neck, sucking up a mark of possession as he thrust into him, making sure to hit just the right spot to make Danny scream as his body erupted. He burned from the inside out until the inferno consumed him and the world went dark.

KIER LAY with Danny in his arms, struggling to catch his breath. He'd wanted this with Danny for so long and to finally get it.... He couldn't find the words. They'd turned a corner with this moment, and it would live in his heart forever.

"Oh my God, Kier. That was.... Whatever the hell it was, it needs to happen more often." He sucked in air between each word as though he'd just finished running a marathon.

Kier smiled and laughed as he rolled his head to the side to look at Danny. When he saw his lover's face, his smile dropped. His beautiful man watched him with a look of sheer bliss on his face and a thin red line trailing toward the corner of his lip.

"Danny, love, your nose is bleeding." Kier eased his arm from beneath Danny's head, then rolled over to grab a handful of tissues.

"What?" Danny reached up to wipe at his nose with a finger. He pulled back his hand and stared at his finger coated in blood. "What the hell?" He pushed himself upright and took Kier's offering, wiping blood from his finger, then dabbing at his nose. He looked at the bright red staining the stark white of the tissue, his expression blank.

"Kier?" The pitch of Danny's voice rose as all the color drained from his face. He wavered, then collapsed back on the floor. Kier scrambled up, reaching for Danny, shaking him as he called Danny's name.

He leaned in close to his face, checking Danny's breathing, and he pressed his finger to his throat, looking for evidence of a pulse. Both were strong and steady.

"Danny? Come on, love. Wake up. You're scaring me." Kier's heart thundered and he fought to keep panic at bay.

"Fuck. Fuck!" He leapt from the bed, snatched up his clothes, and scrambled into them. Then he went back to Danny and patted his cheek. "Come on, Dan. If you don't wake up in the next three seconds, I'm dragging you to Sharon's office."

He rushed to the bathroom, grabbed an enormous wad of toilet paper, then rushed back into the parlor. He dropped down next to

Danny and wiped at the blood that continued to stream from his nose. *Come on. Wake up, dammit.* Nothing.

He scooped up his phone, then wrapped Danny in a blanket and raced for the garage. He sat Danny in the passenger seat, letting his head tilt forward so he wouldn't choke on blood, then rushed around to the driver's seat. On the way, he punched in the speed dial for Sharon.

"Kier? What's wrong? What's happened now?"

"I have no freaking clue. We were in bed together, his nose started bleeding, and then he passed out. I haven't been able to wake him. We're already on our way to you."

"Okay, I'm out. I was making a small house call. I'll meet you back at the house. Come to the downstairs entrance. You know where it is, right?"

"Yeah, I'll meet you—Shit!"

"What? Take a breath and tell me what's going on now," Sharon asked in a calm, soothing voice.

Kier took a short steadying breath but stomped down on the accelerator, his knuckles going white as he gripped the steering wheel. "He's bleeding from the ear now. What do I do, Sharon? I don't know what's happening to him." He clenched his jaw. He hated that he didn't know what to do, didn't have the answers. If he lost Danny now…. No. He couldn't let that happen. Not when they were finding their way back to each other again.

"Kier? Are you still with me?"

Sharon's barked question pulled him out of his head. "I'm here. I'm a minute from your office. Get here now. He needs you. We need you." He pulled to a stop in the alley behind Sharon's office, shoved the car into park, and climbed out and raced around it at a pace faster than the eye could track. He checked Danny's pulse. *Still breathing. Thank God.* He gathered Danny into his arms, pressed a kiss to his temple, then rushed him inside, praying that Sharon had learned enough to be able to help.

THE NEXT morning Rogan walked into the Purity offices with a mission. He'd arrived early hoping to avoid as many people as possible and made his way up to Lydecker's lab. He rolled his shoulders, trying to keep calm, but his pulse and breathing picked up a little speed despite his efforts. He slipped through the hall, making every effort to look like a man going about his morning routine. He'd left all the security cameras recording. Shutting them down would have looked more suspicious than leaving them on to record him going places that he could access on the average day.

Slipping into the lab, he found the lights and all the machinery up and running but the room empty. *Okay, he's here somewhere. Get a move on, Rogan.* He skirted workbenches and various scientific machinery and made for the computer in the back of the room. He smiled when he saw no password protection on it. Thank God for pseudo luddites. Lydecker used technology in his experiments, but when it came to a simple desktop computer, he tended to grumble about useless machines. Which could mean that Rogan would find nothing. The man did like his pencils and notebooks, after all. He just prayed someone had impressed upon Lydecker the benefit of an electronic backup system.

He sat, flicked his gaze to the door and back at the unsecured computer, and started to dig. Christ, hadn't anyone ever taught the man how to make folders? Lydecker's hard drive contained hundreds of numbered documents with no identifying information.

"Seriously?" Rogan muttered as he pulled out the flash drive he'd brought with him and started copying. For all he knew, these files contained a whole lot of nothing, but there was no time to sort it out now. He started the download and checked the door every few seconds.

"Come on, come on. Slow frigging machine."

He'd gotten the better part of five hundred documents copied when the door opened a crack and someone called out a greeting. "Good morning, Dr. Lydecker."

*Fuck.* He clicked to close any open windows and yanked the drive out of the USB port, praying he hadn't corrupted what information he'd copied, and shoved out of the chair just as Lydecker entered the lab.

"Rogan?" Lydecker furrowed his brow. "What are you doing in here?" His gaze flicked to his computer, then back to Rogan.

"Morning, sir. I was looking for some paper to leave you a note. I wanted you to contact me when you got in."

"You could have left me a voicemail."

"You know how you are with voicemails. I thought you'd like my news sooner than two days from now."

Lydecker gave him a hint of a smile as a gleam of hope slipped into his eyes. "Oh? Does that mean you've got news for me about the subject?"

Rogan pressed his lips together. He hated that. They were talking about a man, a person, and fuck, he really had stopped looking at this as just a job when word choice set him off. He shoved his hands into his pockets to keep them from balling into fists.

"I do, sir." *Forgive me, Danny.* He swallowed down the sickness that rose in his throat "We have located Reynolds. We hope to have him in custody very soon."

"Excellent. We have a lot of work to do, and we can't do it until we can bring him in and help the poor man."

*Help my ass.* Rogan nodded, then excused himself and exited the lab. *Fuck!* He needed to get in touch with Kier and let him know to keep an even closer watch on Danny.


DANNY AWOKE alone, and definitely not in Kier's bed. The light in the room was dim, but not so much that he couldn't see the details surrounding him. Earth-toned walls and carpeting, light wood furniture, a red and gold spread on the bed, and a red ceramic pot that held some green leafy plant sat atop the dresser. Where was he, and what the hell had happened?

He propped himself up on his elbows and racked his brain, trying to recall the events of the night. Then it all flooded back. Watching Kier feed. He clenched his jaw at the memory of Kier's hands and mouth on that woman. Then he closed his eyes and took a deep, settling breath at the memory of what had followed. He smiled. Memories were fine, but he wanted Kier lying next to him. Then it came back to him. The less than stellar ending to what was shaping up to be an excellent night. He'd had a nosebleed. One look at the blood on his fingers, and then the world went black. He hadn't even had time to react at all; a wave of sickness crashed through him, and lights out. Pushing all the way up in bed, he reached to feel around his nose. No blood. He flopped back on the pillow. *Thank God.* But now a whole new crop of questions sprang to mind, and a need to be with Kier flooded through him.

Climbing out of bed, he rose a bit unsteadily on his feet, not quite feeling like himself. First stop, bathroom; next stop, get some answers.

"What do you think you're doing? Get back in bed."

Danny jolted at the sound of Kier's voice, and he slapped a hand to his chest. "Are you trying to give me a heart attack? Where did you come from?"

Kier crossed to him, pulled him in close. "I was in the other room. I heard you moving around and came to check on you. Now get back in bed."

"I have to pee. Then I'll get back in bed. But only if you join me." He leaned up and pressed a kiss to Kier's jawline. Instead of the warm response he hoped for, Kier remained stiff and unyielding.

"What is it? What's wrong?"

Kier shook his head and cupped Danny's elbow. His touch was gentle despite the stiffness of his body. "Hurry up, then get vertical again. You need to rest. Sharon, she's just finishing up something in the lab, and then she'll be over to check on you."

Danny nodded in acknowledgment, then entered the small, brightly lit room and closed the door behind him. When he emerged, Kier was sitting on the bed, worried and lost deep in thought.

Danny crossed to him, standing between his spread thighs. He cupped Kier's chin and urged him to look up at him.

"What is it?"

Kier opened his mouth to speak, then closed it again. Danny took his face between his hands. "Honesty, remember? We promised we'd talk and be open with each other from here on out."

Kier nodded. He rested his hands on Danny's hips. "I'm really not liking these episodes of yours."

"They're not much fun for me either." Danny slid his hand over Kier's, interlaced their fingers. "We'll figure this out."

"We have to, one way or the other."

Waiting much longer didn't seem to be an option for him anymore. He thought about what he'd witnessed tonight. How surprised he was that he didn't find it cringeworthy. Instead, he found it sexy, intimate, and something he just might like to share with Kier for a long time to come. Maybe. Still, the thought of going through life so hated and feared that people wanted to kill you didn't appeal, but then again neither did death or life without Kier.

Kier squeezed his fingers gently, pulling him from his thoughts. He met Kier's eyes, who watched him with a mix of curiosity and wariness. He hated that he'd done that to the man who meant everything to him. Kier did it, lived his life each day despite everything. Maybe with Kier by his side, he could be strong enough. Maybe they could find happiness together. Kier's tugged him closer. He kissed him softly and gently. Passion had no place in this moment. He injected all that he couldn't find the words to express in that kiss, that one point of connection.

"Look who's awake," Sharon said, sweeping into the room. "How are you feeling?"

Danny groaned at the interruption. "I'm okay. Maybe a tad off, but that seems to be going away."

Sharon gave him a small smile; then her face became unreadable. "Well, I have news." Sharon tugged a high-back chair from the corner of the room and sat facing Kier and Danny.

"Good or bad?"

"I suppose that depends on your perspective. I took a fresh blood sample tonight." She shook her head, her expression bleak. Bile rose up Danny's throat, leaving a sour taste in his mouth. He didn't want to hear her news, but he couldn't hide from it either.

"Your body is changing faster then I realized, but the changes aren't normal. I don't know how to describe it, but because of the mutation in the blood of the vampire that attacked you, your turning is abnormal, if you can even fully turn at all on your own. You will, however, keep having these attacks until you're finally turned or...."

"Or I die, right?" The words came out in a whisper.

"I can't be positive, but that's what I suspect. All I know for sure is that the progression of this mutated change won't stop. This isn't a natural turning. I don't believe you'll survive it. I wish I had better news for you, Danny, but the fact is you're an anomaly. You shouldn't exist. Something was off about the vampire that bit you, something unnatural. I'm researching this as fast as I can, but this is so foreign, so unique, it could take me years to understand what's happening."

"And a cure is nowhere in sight, right?"

"Not unless this Rogan that Kier told me about comes through with more information, and even then...." She paused and reached out a hand to pat Danny's arm. "I'm really sorry, Danny. I can't tell you how much. I'll give you guys some time to talk and figure out your next steps. Kier, I want to take a blood sample from you, but that can wait until later. I'll be in the lab if you need me." She rose and left the room, closing the door behind her with a quiet click.

"Thanks," Kier murmured. Then he tugged Danny to him and wrapped him in his arms. Danny returned the embrace, pressing his face into Kier's hair and breathing in the clean scent. "We'll get your healthy again. I promise."

"I know we will." Danny shifted so he could place a soft yet reassuring kiss on Kier's lips. "Come lie down with me. I think we both could use the rest."

Kier nodded, toed off his shoes, and climbed in next to Danny. He pulled him into the crook of his arm. Danny curled in close, resting his head on Kier's broad chest. He let the warmth of his lover seep into him, and his body relaxed. Despite his cozy resting place, he couldn't sleep; too much whirled through his mind. He lay wrapped in Kier's arms and began working out a plan to do what needed to be done.

# CHAPTER 11

FROM THE moment he walked out of Purity headquarters with the flash drive in hand, Rogan's senses went on high alert. Tension coursed through him, keeping his muscles all but quivering all day long. Once the sun set, he'd stopped twitching like a cat hopped up on catnip. He calmed a bit because, within the hour, the drive in his pocket wouldn't be his problem anymore. Once he placed it in Kieran's hands, he'd breathe easy again. Well, easier. Until he assured his brother's safety, he'd stay vigilant.

He didn't kid himself into thinking he'd gotten away clean. That sneaky bitch probably had his ass LoJacked and knew his exact location, maybe even what he'd taken from the lab. Getting the data, getting to the bar, it all seemed too easy to Rogan. He didn't understand Melissa's game. He didn't know why she hadn't come after him yet.

When he'd spoken to his brother earlier, his uneasiness had freaked his little brother out some. He regretted that, but if it made Brian more cautious, he could live with it. Rogan had done this. He'd brought this group into their lives. Time to cut ties. No easy task, not while he knew two innocent lives were at stake.

He waited until well after dark before reaching out to Kier again. This time he parked a block away, then made the call.

"McCade." The deep voice rumbled out of the phone.

"It's Rogan. Are you in the bar?"

"No. Why?"

"I've got something for you. Can you meet me?"

"This isn't the best time."

"I've got your data. If you want it, you need to come get it now." Silence stretched between them.

"How do I know this is on the level?"

"I've got no reason to lie to you. My ass is just as much on the line, maybe more so. I don't think Purity knows about you or your connection to Reynolds. If they did, they'd have already come after you hard. But they know about my family, and if they discover what I've done...."

Again, silence.

"All right. I'll be there in fifteen."

"Thanks. See you then." Rogan disconnected the call and scanned the area. Nothing. Everything looked... normal. He exited his SUV and started toward the bar. He'd be safer sitting inside the building full of vampires than he'd be waiting in his vehicle. As he walked, his breathing and heart rate picked up, and he kept checking all around him. No one approached. People passed him on the sidewalk going about their business, not even acknowledging his presence. He still felt like everyone was looking at him and they all knew what he carried in his pocket. He nodded a greeting at Alex as he entered the bar and headed straight for an empty table on the far wall. He sat and continued to scan, his whole body ready to jump into action at the least provocation.

"Can I get you anything?" Alex asked as she approached him.

"No, thanks. I'm waiting on McCade to get here."

Her eyes narrowed. "Why?"

"He's expecting me."

She raised a brow at him, but then her eyes went wide and she claimed a seat. "Do you have information about my brother?"

He shook his head. "I haven't been able to get back in to check on him. But I do have some information that may help get him out of there. I'll wait for Kieran and go through it all once."

"Let me call him." Alex pulled out her phone. Just as she tapped Kier's speed dial number, all hell broke loose.

"WHEN WE get inside, I want you to head straight to my office and lie down on the couch," Kier growled at Danny as they hurried down the street toward the bar.

"Kier, I'm fine."

Kier snorted and shot a sideways look at Danny.

Danny's hand slipped into his, squeezed. "Okay, then let's just say I'm going to be fine." He bumped his shoulder against Kier's arm.

"You woke up a bit weak and out of sorts. We just barely kept food in you, and you look pale as death. Now please just go to my office and rest."

Danny squeezed his hand and nodded in agreement. Kier took a long, slow breath, and a small knot of tension loosened. "Were you always this stubborn?"

"Yes. Yes, I was. It's part of my charm."

Kier snorted again.

Danny tugged his hand, pulling him to a stop. Kier turned to face him. Danny cupped his face and kissed him, short and soft. Kier touched his forehead to Danny's for a long moment, then pulled back and kissed it. "Let's getting moving." They continued down the street, rounding the corner to the front entrance of the bar. Danny stepped forward to open the door. Before he could grip the handle, his hand slapped at his neck, and then with a gasp he dropped to the ground.

"Danny?" Kier's heart leapt into his throat as he rushed toward him. He crouched next to Danny, then rolled him to his back. His hands rushed over him as he checked his breathing. He placed a finger on his neck to check his pulse and noticed a small dart imbedded in Danny's neck.

"What the hell?" He scowled, tossed the small projectile on the ground, and whipped his gaze up to search the area.

He needed to move. Needed to get both of them to safety. Just as he pushed to his feet, a sharp flare of pain flashed through his neck as a dart struck him.

"Shit." He yanked out the dart, tossing it aside and bending down to grab Danny. When he did his vision blurred, but he needed to move before the drug knocked him out cold. Just a few steps and they'd be inside. He tried to lift Danny's limp body, but weakness spread through him. *Damn, this shit is strong.* His mind started to go foggy. He collapsed and his hand reached out to grip Danny's arm to pull him close. The bar door opened and someone shouted for help. People started pouring out of the bar, and an explosion of gunfire rang out.

"Help us get inside," he rasped out, but no one heard him. Bullets pinged off concrete and brick, and chaos erupted. People panicked and ran, even if that led them into the line of fire. *We're going to get trampled* flitted across his mind even as the crowd of people scattered like pool balls. For one split second, his vision cleared. A man and woman both clad in black approached them. The man crouched over Danny as though intending to offer aid. The woman stared down at Kier with more hate in her eyes than he'd ever had thrown at him in his life. The man hefted Danny over his shoulder. In his mind Kier screamed and cursed, and he commanded his body to move, to fight, but the tranquilizer kept his body from responding. As the pair disappeared into the darkness with Danny, Kier slipped into oblivion.

"KIER? CAN you hear me?"

Kier furrowed his brow. He wanted to sink back into the darkness and hide away from the buzzing and pounding in his head, but fought his way back to consciousness instead. He swatted at the annoyance that kept shaking him and calling his name. He knew that voice. He followed it out from underneath the drug-induced haze and back into reality.

"Kier? You back with me?"

He croaked out his friend's name as he eased open an eye and squinted at the room. Alex studied his face with worried eyes; Rogan's expression remained stoic. He scanned the room. His office. Alex had managed to drag him in here and laid him on the couch. He pushed himself on his elbows.

"Easy." Alex moved to help him. "Take your time. How do you feel? Headache?"

"I'm fine." He squinted against the hammering in his head. "What the hell did they shoot me with? Tranquilizers don't usually affect me that fast, but this dropped me almost as soon as I was hit."

"That's Purity R&D at work. I told you, they've got an arsenal full of weapons like you've never seen before. Looks like their new sedative dart is very effective. Now that they've learned a bit more about vampire metabolism, they've been tinkering with the dosage so that it takes effect faster."

"Shit." Kier eased himself into a sitting position, looked around the room again, and froze. His body tensed, breath dammed in his lungs. "Where's Danny? How long was I out?" He shot to his feet, then dropped back down onto the chair when the room spun.

"The sedative put you down for about two hours. It's about nine o'clock."

"Danny?"

Alex and Rogan glanced at each other, then back at Kier. Rogan crossed his arms and stared down at his feet. "I'm sorry, Kier. They took him. Melissa and her minions. They've got him inside Purity's compound as we speak."

Kier roared out the rage, desperation, and fear that rampaged through him, but it was Alex who grabbed Rogan's black T-shirt in her fist, lifted him, then got in his face. She shook him as she growled at him. "What did you do? Did you betray us to Purity?" She looked over at Kier. "I told you we couldn't trust his ass."

Rogan clutched at her wrist, struggling to be freed. "It's not what you think. If you'll put me down, I'll explain."

She glanced at Kier again, and he nodded. She dropped Rogan, crossed her arms, and glared at him.

Rogan rubbed at his neck and cleared his throat. Then he reached into his pocket and pulled out a flash drive. "I got caught by Lydecker as I was leaving his lab with this. This drive contains all of his notes on his computer. I don't know what is what because nothing was labeled. There's no file called 'the cure for vampirism.' Hopefully, there is something on here that can help Reynolds. After we get him back, of course."

"You got caught. What does that mean? Did they send you in here after Danny?" With a burst of speed, Kier stood toe to toe with Rogan, glaring into cool blue eyes.

He eased back from Kier. "No. I didn't betray your trust... entirely."

"Explain!"

Rogan held up his hands to protect himself when Kier lunged. "Not the throat again. I can't talk if you keep strangling me."

"Then start fucking talking. Fast."

"Lydecker walked in as I was trying to leave his lab. The only way I could get out of there clean was to tell him I'd come to report progress. I told him we'd found Reynolds and would be bringing him in soon."

"Could he have sent his own soldiers and not waited for you? Before I passed out, I saw two armed, black-clad people approaching us. One man, one woman."

"No. I never gave him a location."

"So how did he find us?"

"I don't think he did. I think Melissa tracked me here. She was desperate to get to Reynolds. It's just like her to grab him like this."

"Fuck! Will she kill him?" A wave of cold washed over Kier, and a queasy sensation settled into his stomach at the thought of Danny being tortured and killed while Kier fought to get to him. He wiped a hand over his mouth.

"She will, yes. How quickly I can't say. I know she planned to lock him in with Aiden, but beyond that I don't know. So we need to move fast. You're going to need my help to get into the compound." He nodded at the computer on Kier's desk. "May I?" He pulled another flash drive out of his pocket. "I've got the building schematics on this."

Kier studied him. "How do I trust you?"

When the silence stretched, Rogan rolled his eyes and spoke. "Accept the fact that you're going to have to trust me because I'm your only way in and out of the Purity compound."

Kier hesitated for a long moment. "Fine. Let's see what you've got."

Rogan crossed to the desk, claiming the chair. "I'm hoping Melissa hasn't revoked my clearances yet, but even if she has, it doesn't matter. She's not the only one who knows how to put a backup plan in place." Rogan loaded up the plans. "Okay, Lydecker's lab is here. Melissa's lab is here. Aiden's cell is at the far end near a secondary exit that only opens with a retinal scan. So, once you get him out, you'll have to backtrack up the stairs to get out of the building."

Alex leaned closer to see the screen. "There's nothing there but a corridor and utility pipes."

"That's because Melissa somehow managed to alter the plans. I assure you the lab and an alternate exit out of the building are located in that space. On the main level, exits are here, here, and here. There are stairwells here and here." Rogan tapped the screen as he pointed to the various locations. "Once you're inside, we're going to have to move fast and cover a lot of ground."

"How do we know which lab Danny's in?"

"I'll try and confirm, but while you were still out cold, I called in to the guards on shift and let them know to make Lydecker aware that Reynolds was en route. I'm gambling that Reynolds's chances are better with the good doctor than the crazy bitch. If all went to plan, he'll be in this lab here on the top floor." Rogan stabbed at another room on the map.

"Okay, we know where we need to go once we get in the building. How do we get onto the property?" Alex asked.

"This means we'll have to divide and conquer. I'll head in so that I can clear you through the gates. Once you're in, I'll shut down the cameras and the electric locking system. If you get caught while you're in there.... Just don't get caught. Understood?"

Kier nodded.

"The guard schedules are usually lightest around two in the morning. That gives us a few hours to get ourselves together and for me to get in place. I'll text you if anything changes or Danny's or Aiden's... status changes."

"You mean if they get killed before we get there," Alex snapped, but worry shined in her eyes.

Rogan rose from the desk chair, lifted his hand, hesitated, then laid it on Kier's shoulder. "Good luck to all of us." He strode out of the office.

Kier collapsed into his desk chair, his legs unable to hold him up anymore. His head dropped into his hands. He didn't want to imagine Danny's treatment at the hands of Purity's zealots.

Alex rubbed his shoulders. "He's going to be all right. We'll get him out of there."

"He could already be dead. If that woman wants him dead...."

"But if Rogan is right and this Lydecker guy gets his hands on Danny, he's got a fighting chance. Let's agree to assume that, until we hear otherwise from Rogan, Danny and Aiden are still alive. I need your head in this, Kier. Danny needs your head in this."

Kier dragged his hands through his hair. He closed his eyes and gathered all the fear and worry and wrapped it in the thick layer of cold, focused anger. Damn right Kier would bring Danny out alive. He'd tear the limbs off anyone who got in his way. "We'll get them both out. One way or another."

Alex hugged him. Kier squeezed her tight in return. They would all get through this. He couldn't think otherwise.

The tight knot of dread that sat heavy in Kier's stomach since he'd awakened to find Danny gone, eased. *Hang in there, love. I'm coming to get you.*


THE DULL, unrelenting throbbing in his head pulled Danny out of the darkness and back into consciousness. He took internal stock of his body. No pain anywhere else—that was a good sign. The fact that he'd had another episode was a bad sign. He eased his eyes open and rolled his head to the side since lifting it took a level of energy he didn't have at the moment.

"Oh God, where am I? How did I get here?" He whispered the words, praying he didn't get an answer. Dim light came from a single source. It illuminated a high-tech science lab that outshined Dr. Sharon's lab by a mile. All manner of machines filled the large room. Little red and green glowing lights decorated their surfaces, making Danny think of creatures watching him from the darkness. Creatures that might be able to do unspeakable things to him. He shuddered and his stomach clenched as a coil of sickness wound its way through him, leaving a bitter taste in the back of his throat. The sudden pain in his neck when he stood outside of the Haven came back to him. Oh God, he hadn't had another episode. He'd been kidnapped.

He jerked his head in the other direction, wanting a full view of his surroundings, and froze. Everything in him iced over. His breath clogged his lungs. On the table next to him lay a selection of needles, scalpels, and implements of pain and destruction. *Oh fuck. Oh fuck. Oh fuck. Purity.* Somehow they'd found him. *Oh damn, I am in so much trouble.*

Danny jerked. *Kier!* Blood rushed through his body, the roar in his ears deafening. He tried to rise but found himself restrained. He lifted his head and searched the room as best he could, squinting to see into the shadows. "Kier?" Silence. *Please, God, let him be all right.* Purity could have only gotten to him if Kier were unconscious or…. He couldn't think it. If those bastards laid a finger on Kier…. A sob escaped him as panic screamed in his head. He struggled against the leather four-point restraints to no avail.

"Mr. Reynolds, please settle yourself."

Cold spread along Danny's extremities at the sound of the soft words. The owner probably meant for it to be soothing, but he failed miserably. A tall, lanky man in green scrubs emerged from the darkness. Light glinted off the metal rim of his glasses, hiding his eyes behind the glare.

"Who are you? I demand you release me right now." Danny tried to keep his tone neutral but couldn't stop the slight break in his voice.

The man smiled at his words, but it held no warmth. Danny clenched his body, fighting back the urge to tremble.

"Now as I was saying, it's so nice of you to join me, Mr. Reynolds. I wasn't sure how long it was going to take the effects of the drug to wear off as you were given a full vampire dose of the tranquilizer. I've been very anxious to meet you. In fact, I've been trying to arrange a meeting for a few days." The man walked to the side of the table. He stood, staring down at Danny, his hands shoved into the pockets of his lab coat.

"You're the one who sent men to my apartment to kidnap me. Who the hell are you? What gives you the right?"

"My name is Dr. Thomas Lydecker, chief scientist and cofounder of Purity. It's a great pleasure to meet you finally. I was so excited to hear that Rogan had located you and even more so when I learned that you were being brought in."

Danny clenched his jaw. "Yeah, yeah, nice to meet you. Get to the point. What the fuck do you want?"

Lydecker tsked. "Such language." He shook his head and crossed to a plexiglass wall mount that held boxes of nitrile gloves. He extracted two and slid them on his hands. "You, sir, are going to aid me in the completion of my research. All of those lovely little cells running through your veins hold the answers that I've been seeking for years."

"So, all I need to do is give you a few vials of blood and I can be on my way?"

Lydecker barked out a humorless laugh. "I'm afraid I need more than that." Lydecker walked in slow circles around the table, hands clasped behind his back, his tone calm and cold.

"See, I recently lost my test subject, but you should know that. After all, you were the source of his demise. That vampire you killed was my son, Jared." Lydecker uttered the last few words low and menacing. When Lydecker spoke again, he once again used that cordial, measured tone. "Thank you, by the way, for leaving a sample of your blood behind so that we could identify you."

The man stood at the foot of the table studying Danny like the experiment he'd become. *Oh God, I need to get the hell out of here. Now!* Danny struggled, pulling against his restraints, knowing he couldn't loosen them, but unwilling to lie there and let the crazy man start extracting bits and pieces of him to make slides.

"While my heart breaks from the loss, my son isn't gone. He lives on in you. His blood cells flow through your veins, have merged with your cells. Together you have brought me that much closer to a cure."

Bile burned its way up Danny's throat. "You experimented on your own child? What kind of monster does that?"

Lydecker shifted his gaze to the floor, and for a moment he appeared lost in his own thoughts. His voice was soft when he spoke again. "As distasteful as it may have seemed, it was a necessary evil. I had to run tests. Had to know if my drug worked, and what a crowning achievement it would have been to have my own son be the very first cured vampire. Saved from that horrid existence. Saved from his own poor decisions."

"Poor decisions?"

Lydecker nodded. "My Jared had a bit of a rebellious streak that we never could manage to rein in. He let himself be turned. Allowed himself to be violated and tainted. I had to save him from himself." He met Danny's eyes again, the look in them a bit manic. "Together Jared and I would have spearheaded the movement to cure the poor, unfortunate creatures afflicted with this terrible disease. Forced to drink blood, live a life without morals, without thought or care for other beings." His lip curled up into a sneer.

Danny's breathing got loud, his chest heaving. He couldn't stop the words that spewed from his mouth. "Necessary evil, my ass. You did it for your own glorification. Your own bigotry. Did you ever stop to think that vampires are happy the way they are? They don't want to be *cured*, don't need it. Have you ever met a vampire outside of your son? Most are just like everyone else. They just want to live their lives. You, Purity, the whole lot of you. You have no right to decide how anyone should live, and you certainly don't have the right to force your opinions, or your so-called cures, on others." Again he tugged at the unbreakable restraints.

Lydecker's eyes narrowed. "That, my dear boy, is a matter for debate, but enough chat. It's time we got started." Lydecker walked to the tool tray, studied the array of instruments. *Oh God, oh God, get me out of here now!* His eyes went wide and his heart tried to pound its way out of his chest as Lydecker selected a small, flexible plastic tool. For the most part it looked innocuous enough, except for the blade attached to the length of it. He'd never seen anything like it before, but he was not eager to find out how it worked.

"Aren't you supposed to anesthetize me first?"

Lydecker held the device between his thumb and index finger and flexed it a few times. "It would be only fair that you share in the pain that my son experienced the night you killed him. The night you took him from me. Now let's start with a skin sample and go from there, shall we?"

# CHAPTER 12

AT ONE forty-five in the morning, Rogan marched into the security control room at Purity. Kier and Alex were on their way, and he needed to make some adjustments to the security cameras before they arrived. When he entered he found one man asleep in his chair and the other facedown in a book.

"Good evening, gentlemen." Both men snapped to attention. The chair the sleeping man had occupied fell backward, clattering to the floor.

"Sir!" Both men shot him worried glances as though waiting for a dressing down.

"Night shift sucks, doesn't it?" Rogan smiled. "Why don't you go take a break. Get some coffee. I'll keep an eye on the monitors for the next fifteen."

"Yes, sir. Thank you, sir." The two men didn't wait for Rogan to ask twice. They rushed from the room and down the hall. Rogan shut and locked the door behind them. He leaned against it and blew out a relieved breath. Then he pulled out his phone and dialed.

"Kier? It's Rogan. You're cleared to enter through the rear gate. At this hour, it's ID card access only. As soon as I see you approach on the camera, I'll raise the gate. I'll meet you by the rear fire entrance, next to the large junction box."

"Got it."

"Once you're in, move fast, and if you get caught, you're on your own."

"Understood."

As the call ended Rogan did a quick sweep of the monitors to get a general idea of people's positions throughout the building. Melissa Moran emerged from the stairwell onto the level that housed Dr. Lydecker's lab. Even through the camera Rogan could see waves of fury rising off her like thermal waves off hot pavement. The look on her face was one of pure rage and hatred as she marched down the hall toward the lab.

"Oh shit." Just as she disappeared into Lydecker's lab, Kier's car pulled up to the gate. Rogan coded him in and rushed from the room, heading for the designated meeting place. The faster he got them in, the faster they could all get out and away. Rogan wouldn't breathe easy until all of them were safely out of this place.

DANNY LAY panting on the table as beads of sweat and tears rolled down his face into his hair. The pain had stopped for the interim while the sadistic bastard holding him hostage started his army of scientific machinery on their mission to gather information about what made him tick.

*Please God, let Kier be okay and on his way.* Danny looked toward the lab doors, praying that at any moment it would burst open. He wanted to see Kier or Alex standing there, but he'd settle for Rogan or anyone who could make the pain stop. He didn't know if he could stand to have one more "sample" collected. If Lydecker came near him with a scalpel again, he might lose his mind.

"How are we doing so far, Daniel? Good?"

"I'm not good, you sadistic fuck."

Lydecker's tone went flat and cold. "I've warned you about language once already. You won't like what happens if I have to do it again."

Danny squeezed his eyes closed as his heart slammed against his rib cage. He huffed out a laugh. "You're slicing bits and pieces off me to do your crazy little experiments on, but it's my language that's the biggest concern. Seriously?"

"Come now, it hasn't been bad, and we're just getting started."

Danny tossed a wide-eyed look at Lydecker. His eyes went even wider when Lydecker selected a syringe containing a pale yellow liquid off the instrument tray and approached the table.

Danny went still.

Lydecker pressed on the plunger of the syringe until a few drops of the liquid emerged from the tip of the needle. "This is the latest version of my serum. I never got a chance to test its effectiveness. No, you deprived me and my son of that opportunity. But at least before he left this world he gave me the gift of you. So, now you'll get to experience the benefits of my hard work."

Lydecker grabbed his arm and located a vein. He pinned Danny's arm to the table as he inserted the needle and began to inject.

"Oh fuck!" Danny cried out as the serum burned its way up his arm, the pain so great it stole his breath. He clenched his teeth as waves of searing agony rolled through him.

"With a little drug, the solution should start reversing what was begun with my son's bite."

Danny screamed; then his muscles started twitching and jerking. All thought slid from his head as he did his best to ride out the misery.

"Well, this isn't good." Lydecker stood over him, studying him like a bug under a microscope. He pulled out his notebook and began writing in it.

When the spasms subsided, Danny lay there sucking in great gulps of air, his body trembling, the taste of blood from where he'd bitten his tongue filling his mouth. Lydecker put down his notebook and picked up another syringe. "Just one more quick sample. Hold still now."

*Fucker.* He couldn't have lifted his arm if his life depended on it.

At this point Danny didn't even wince when the needle slid into his arm. *Please. Please.*

When the door opened, a jolt of excitement shot through him, just to die like water poured on an ember. A woman stood in the doorway. She wore a black turtleneck, tactical pants, and a frown. She'd pulled her hair back in a high ponytail and all but shot lasers out of her eyes at Lydecker. Fury radiated from every inch of her body.

"Good evening, Melissa. Come to see what progress I've made with my research? The combination of Daniel's blood and Jared's generated some fascinating results. I'm fairly certain that I am closer than I've ever been to a cure."

He turned back to his instrument table and picked up more blood vials. *Oh God. This man is going to drain me dry.* Danny didn't miss the irony of the situation.

Melissa stepped into the room and shoved the door closed behind her. "I don't give a shit about your useless experiments that have been nothing but a waste of this organization's time and resources. I've had enough."

Lydecker rounded to face Melissa. "What on earth has gotten into you? My work is vital to fulfilling Purity's mission."

She spat out a laugh. "You don't even know what Purity's mission is anymore. This organization isn't about curing the sick. We're about protecting the world from a menace. We're about wiping the impure from the face of the earth. Not giving them a pill and hoping it works. There is only one way to completely kill a cancer, and that's to cut it out." Her voice rose as she spoke so that by the end, she all but shouted. Disgust dripped from every word.

"You have lost your mind and a clear understanding of our mission. Our goal has always been to heal those afflicted with this condition. No one could possibly want to live their life that way. I brought you into this organization because I thought you and I had a similar vision for the future, but clearly I was wrong. But if that's what you truly believe, then you don't belong here, and I'll have to ensure that you are removed from any position of power within the organization immediately."

Danny tried to flatten himself on the table and become as small as possible. All they were missing was the soundtrack from *The Good, the Bad, and the Ugly*. These two were about to have a showdown at high noon, and Danny didn't want to get caught in the crossfire. Sure enough, Melissa reached behind her back and retrieved a small-caliber gun with an attached silencer.

*Fuck! Not good.* Danny held his breath and went as still as possible, trying not draw Melissa's attention. She advanced on Lydecker, who backed away, moving deeper into the lab until she'd trapped him between a wall and a lab table.

"Melissa, let's calm down. We can talk this out. I think you can still play a vital role in Purity, but it should be a different role than the one you're currently fulfilling, that's all. There's no need to resort to anger and violence."

"We're going to have to agree to disagree, Doctor." She raised the gun and pulled the trigger, firing twice. The doctor didn't utter another word. He collapsed to the floor in a spreading pool of blood. Then she turned and her cold, flat eyes landed on Danny. A small, evil smile spread across her lips.

Danny flattened himself against the table; he didn't move, didn't blink. A cold sweat erupted over his body.

"Mr. Reynolds, I've been looking for you. You were quite elusive for a while there, but thanks to that bastard Rogan, I tracked you down. Oh, he did his best to keep you away from me, and he'll have to pay for his betrayal, and yet here we are." She swaggered her way toward him, tapping the gun against her palm.

*Oh fuck.* He didn't want to die. He wanted to see Kier again. Hold him. Build a life with him.

"You have been nothing but a problem for me. And now we're going to fix that."

"Come on, you really don't want to do this."

She stared at him a moment, then turned away. Danny furrowed his brow. He'd been preparing to be shot any second, not for her to walk away from him. She crossed the room heading for a glass-fronted cabinet that held bottles of assorted chemicals. After tugging open the doors, she grabbed bottles at random and started pouring the contents around the lab, ringing his table with liquid and drenching Lydecker's body.

"I've done nothing to you. Why are you doing this?"

"It may not have been intentional, but you've caused me more problems than you know. At first, you did me a favor. You killed Jared and with his death, Lydecker's quest for a cure should have ended. But it didn't and here we are."

"What did I ever do to you? I didn't ask for any of this to happen to me. I'm just trying to live my life just like anyone else."

"You've been infected—not your fault, which is unfortunate, but surely you understand why I can't let you live. It's really the best thing for you. Death is a far better option than living life as one of these vile creatures. Plus, Lydecker and all aspects of his research need to go. That includes you. His death will be attributed to a tragic accident. I will step into his shoes and lead this organization in a new direction. The true direction. The world must be made to understand the danger vampires pose to us. They are unnatural predators, and they need to be put down so that they can never destroy another family."

Melissa walked from lab table to lab table, turning knobs until gas hissed out of each spigot.

Danny's mind churned, searching for any way to keep her from burning this room down around him. "I get it, I do. My brother was attacked by a vampire, and he's gone through hell trying to recover."

"Then you get it. You get why there is no place in our world for beasts who take pleasure in the pain and fear and death of humans."

"I don't understand. What's so bad about curing vampires? Doesn't that give you exactly what you want?"

Melissa whirled, eyes narrowed. "You have no idea what I want. Lydecker never could understand that once tainted, always tainted. These monsters, they stole my family. Bastards turned my husband into one of them, and they locked me in the room with him to be his first feed after his change. I was already weak from being their human buffet before they stuck me in that room to be drained by my own husband. They left me tied to a chair. I broke the chair to free myself. While the man that I'd loved, who had loved me for seven years lay there becoming a monster, I shoved a broken chair leg through his heart."

Danny almost felt sorry for her. He pitied her for what she'd endured, an event that so clearly fractured her mental health. But he couldn't quite dig up any sympathy for someone who wanted to turn him into a charred husk.

"It was better. He wouldn't have wanted to live that way. No sane person would." Her voice quavered. She strolled to Lydecker's desk and snatched up his notebook. She walked to Lydecker's lifeless body, pulled a lighter from her pocket, and with the flick of her thumb, set the pages ablaze. Then she dropped the burning notebook onto Lydecker's chest. Flames erupted with a loud whump.

"Goodbye, Reynolds. It's been interesting." She departed the room, leaving Danny screaming for help and fighting his bindings with everything he had in him.

ROGAN HUSTLED through the corridors, slipping into the stairwell and jogging down the two flights of stairs that would lead him to the rear emergency exit. He stood for a moment listening for the sound of feet on concrete and found himself alone. He pushed the door open and let Kier and Alex into the building. They slipped in and pulled the door closed behind them carefully so it would latch without a sound.

In hushed tones, Rogan gave instructions. "Okay, Alex, the door to the lab where Aiden is being held is one flight down. Take a left once you exit the stairway, another left at the end of that corridor. The door to the lab is in that hall. You can't miss it—it's the first door on the right once you make that second turn. It's a low-traffic floor, so you shouldn't encounter anyone. I couldn't get the code from Melissa, so I hope you have a way to get in."

Alex rolled her shoulders. "Please. I won't need a code to get through the door."

"Stay safe." Kier laid a hand on her shoulder. Alex nodded, then without a sound, she disappeared down the stairs.

Rogan turned his attention to Kier. "Follow me. You'd wind up lost in the building trying to find Lydecker's lab."

"Cameras?" Kier asked.

"Already taken care of. I put the cameras in the main surveillance room on a video loop. Rerouted the live streams to my phone." He pulled out his phone and tapped on an app that pulled up the security camera feeds, in particular the feed that focused on the exterior of Lydecker's lab. All clear.

Kier leaned in to look over his shoulder. "Impressive."

"Thanks. It helps to have a little brother who knows way too much about electronics." He smirked, then nodded at the door. "Let's go. I haven't seen anyone in that hall for a while, but I haven't had my eye on the monitor the whole time. We need to be careful and quiet."

"What's that?" Kier gestured at something on the screen.

Rogan zoomed the image and watched a tendril of smoke creep out from under the door. "Fuck, we need to move." He took off up the stairs with Kier on his heels. He swiped to enter onto the top floor. The door released with a soft click.

They rushed through the door and moved as fast as they could along the twisting network of halls that lead to Lydecker's lab.

"I'm surprised you haven't been locked out of the system."

Rogan glanced back at Kier. "I never expected to not get caught. But I make it a goal to always have, at least, a plan B. Plus I made a master key a while ago. Never leave home without it." Rogan shot Kier a smile.

Keir rolled his eyes.

"Melissa will realize I have one eventually, but by then it won't matter anymore. After tonight, I won't need it."

When they arrived outside of the lab, thicker plumes of smoke escaped the room along with an acrid chemical odor. Danny's shouts for help sounded from within.

"I'm coming for you, Danny. Hang on, love," Kier yelled as he lunged for the door.

"Kier! Oh, thank you. I can't get out. I'm still tied down in here."

Rogan placed his hand on the door and assessed the temperature. "It's not hot. Okay, let's move. I don't think we should breathe the air in there for too long."

Easing the door open, they pushed their way into a lab rapidly filling with smoke and flame.

"Get Danny. I'm going to see if I can put out these flames."

With a nod, Kier rushed to Danny and freed the man from his restraints. "I've got you, love. We're going to get you out here." Kier's voice stayed calm despite the chaos surrounding them.

Danny groaned as Kier lifted him from the table. "Rogan, be careful." Danny croaked out the words. "She turned on the gas and doused the floor with chemicals."

Rogan lifted his hand in acknowledgment as he moved to grab a fire extinguisher off the wall. He blasted at the flames as he tried to get to all the open gas valves, coughing as the smoke and chemical vapors burned his nose and throat. He turned off as many of the valves as he could, but the flames continued to rage on. That's when he noticed Lydecker lying among the flames. "Shit."

"Rogan, let's go. He's dead. There's nothing more we can do for him," Kier called to him as he hefted Danny into his arms.

Rogan stared down at the man, a complex mix of emotions welling up inside. Lydecker's death meant that a powerful force of bigotry had fallen. But he couldn't help but pity the father whose grief had driven him to extremes.

Glass exploded and Rogan flinched, raising his arms to cover his face. "Time to get out of here." He turned toward Kier and Danny and together they rushed toward the door.

They exited the lab and sealed the doors shut behind them.

Kier carried Danny as he rushed down the hall toward the stairwell.

"Thank God you came." Danny mumbled the words into Kier's neck.

"I'm so damn sorry, love. So sorry. We're going to get you home and patched up in no time."

"This way." As Rogan guided them through the maze of corridors, he pulled up the security app and tried to activate the sprinkler system, but it didn't respond to his commands. He tried to switch back to the security feeds, but they wouldn't load.

"I think I've been locked out of the system. We better move. Stay close. I don't know where anyone is now."

"Kier, put me down. I can walk. You need your hands free just in case."

Rogan did a quick visual catalog of Danny's injuries. Blood oozing from numerous cuts, bruising around his wrists from the restraints. His eyes were sunken. He looked pale, he wore a grimace of pain, and soot and sweat covered him from head to toe. Danny Reynolds looked like he'd been put through hell.

"Dan, I think we'll move faster if you let Kier carry you. You're not exactly looking your best right now."

"Don't worry about me. I can manage." Kier kissed Danny's temple, and they kept moving.

Rogan stayed vigilant, watching for any security patrols making the rounds. When they made the final turn that led to the stairwell, their luck ran out. Five soldiers waited for them, guns at the ready.

"Sir, I need you to drop your weapons and put your hands up."

"Rogan, can't you call them off?" Danny whispered.

"I can try." He raised his hands and took a step forward. "Lower your weapons, men. You have no authority to stop us. Stand down and let us through."

"I'm sorry, sir, but our orders come directly from Ms. Moran. We are not to let any of you leave the premises."

"I see. You've got your orders. I understand. But, maybe we can put off the detainments until we all get out of this building? Lydecker is dead. His lab is burning as we speak, and the sprinklers aren't turning on. With all the gases and chemicals in that room, this entire floor will become a fireball any minute now." Rogan caught the nervous glances among the four troops who had yet to say anything, so he pushed. "You're going to get these men hurt or killed if we don't get out of the building now." More nervous fidgeting.

"Nice try, Rogan, but we're not buying it." But Rogan heard the thread of doubt that belied the tough stance. "You probably killed Lydecker yourself helping your little freak-of-nature friends try to escape. Besides, Ms. Moran has regained control of the security systems that you tampered with. If there really were a fire, she would have already activated the fire suppression system."

Rogan let his arms drop to his sides. "You moron. She killed Lydecker and started the fire herself. She's not going to stop it. She wants it to burn." More nervous glances and fidgeting. Rogan noted that one solder took a step back toward the doors.

"Enough! I'm through talking. On your knees, hands behind your heads, all of you."

Rogan lowered his voice and turned his head but kept one eye on the soldiers. "No talking our way out of this one."

"Okay, here we go." Kier breathed out the words. "Can you stand?" he whispered to Danny.

"Yeah."

Kier eased Danny to his feet. "Stay back. Stay safe." Then he angled in front of him.

They complied with the soldier's instructions, watching and waiting as all five slowly approached. When they were within arm's reach, Rogan sprang into action. With a few precision moves, he'd taken out the soldier closest to him and started for the next. Kier became a flurry of motion, at times moving so fast his progress couldn't be tracked by the naked eye.

Rogan stayed out of Kier's way. Instead, he guarded Danny, who'd crouched down and huddled against the wall. He didn't look well at all. What the hell had Lydecker done to him?

Bodies flew and shots rang out. In a matter of minutes, silence fell throughout the hall again. Kier had taken out four members of a five-man team of trained operatives.

"Well, shit." Rogan took in the sight of bodies strewn across the hall in crumpled heaps. "Damn, Kier."

"Admire later. Grab their weapons now."

"Think we should restrain them?"

"No. I want them to be able to get out when they come to, but I don't want them sneaking up on me with a weapon."

Together Rogan and Kier started to disarm the men when an explosion rocked the floor and smoke came streaming around the corner.

"Time to go," Kier said.

Danny tried to stand but collapsed again, his body tensed with pain. Kier bent to help him up. He paused, winced.

"Kier, are you okay?" Danny looked up at him with wide eyes.

"Kier, you're bleeding." Rogan laid a hand on his back. "Did you get hit?"

"Bullet grazed me along the rib cage. Burns like a son of a bitch, but it will calm down in a minute. We need to keep going." Kier reached for Danny again and scooped him into his arms. "We'll move faster if I carry you. Let's get out of this place, and then we'll worry about our variety pack of injuries."

Danny relented with a nod. The three rushed into the stairwell and raced down the stairs.

"Hang in there for me," Kier murmured to Danny.

"I'll be all right. In fact, I'm starting to feel better."

When they reached the ground floor exit, Kier set Danny down. "Rogan, do me a favor. Take Danny, head for your car. I'll go find Alex and Aiden."

Danny wrapped his arms around Kier. "No, I'm not leaving without you."

Rogan shook his head. "Nope. We stick together. We're stronger together."

"Fine. Which way to the lab?"

Rogan lead them down two more floors. They raced down the hall to the underground lab. As they made the last turn, Alex and Aiden emerged past the mangled metal door.

Something in Rogan loosened at seeing Aiden alive, if not well.

Alex smiled at Rogan. "I told you I didn't need any damn code."

"Damn, Alex."

"I was motivated." She hugged her arm tighter around her brother.

The five of them made their way back to the rear emergency exit of the building. Rogan hit the lever to open the door that led out of the building to freedom. As soon as they hit the exterior, they found Melissa and a force of at least twenty-five men waiting for them.

"Well, shit."

# CHAPTER 13

"ROGAN, ROGAN, Rogan" Melissa smiled, dark and dangerous. "Did you really think it would be that easy? You must take me for a fool. Granted I should have realized your betrayal sooner. Should have smelled the filth on you, but we all make mistakes."

"Melissa, don't do this. Just let us go and no one else needs to get hurt."

"You know better than that. You know I can't just let you walk away. I've got plans for Purity now that our fearless leader is no longer with us, and you and your associates have made yourselves a danger to my plans. You and your associates are liabilities. You understand?"

Rogan snorted. "It's just business, right?"

"It's mostly business. See, you broke the rules, Rogan. You turned your back on your family here at Purity. We can't let people think you can just walk away and that there will be no consequences."

"Seriously?" Rogan barked out a laugh as his stomach jittered. "This is a job. It's a paycheck. It's not a cult or a secret society. You really have lost your mind."

Melissa leveled a cold hard glare on Rogan and pointed her gun at him. "I think we're done here. Take them."


"WHAT THE hell are we going to do, Kier?" Alex stepped closer to him and spoke in hushed tones.

Kier's gaze swept across the wall of soldiers. Twenty-five soldiers versus two vampires and a human. He didn't like those odds, but he wouldn't let these people get their hands on his family.

"Damn, these guys are like roaches. They come out in darkness, and you just can't get rid of them," Alex muttered. "How are we going to get out of here?"

Rogan had moved in front of the group to confront Melissa. Kier didn't want to pull her focus. "Rogan, stay where you are and just listen. Keep her talking for as long as you can. When we give the word, Alex and I are going to split the field. Alex, you take the left. I'll go right. Rogan, you hang back a bit and take out as many soldiers as you can. Alex and I can move fast and avoid getting overwhelmed in a large crowd of attackers. Your job is to defend Aiden and Danny and to be our eyes scanning the whole field. Wiggle your finger if you understand."

Rogan acknowledged and kept his attention on Melissa.

"What about me? Three vampires are better than two."

"Aiden, I need you to stay with Danny. Once the fighting starts, I want you and Danny to duck behind the junction box. Once we clear a path, head for the van and get it started." Kier let the keys dangle from his fingers.

"No way. These bastards owe me."

"You're not up to full steam yet. Just do as you're told. Please." Alex shot an annoyed look at her brother.

Danny stepped forward and pressed against Kier's back. "Kier, I can defend myself."

"I know, love, but I need to know you're safe. If you're with Aiden, I know you'll be okay."

Danny blew out a breath but nodded in agreement. Aiden stepped next to Kier and took the van keys.

Danny squeezed Kier's arm even as his heart rate sped up and his mouth went dry. "Kier, please be careful."

Kier covered Danny's hand with his own. "I'll be fine. You be safe. When it's clear, head straight for the van. All right? I need to know you're safe."

"All of you freeze. Drop your weapons and put your hands up," the unit commander yelled across the open space.

"Fuck you!" Rogan yelled.

"Let's do this. Now." At Kier's words, the group lunged into action.

DANNY AND Aiden huddled behind the large junction box and watched the action. In a burst of dizzying motion, the two vampires were on the men, cutting through them like a mower over grass.

Danny saw Alex drop a guard while looking like something out of *Crouching Tiger, Hidden Dragon*. She did a flying back kick and sent a soldier airborne, landing a few feet away from Kier. Kier was pure street fighter. Quick, smart, and no holds barred.

He slammed a fist into the man in front of him, putting the guard down for the count and opening the gap that he and Aiden needed to get to their vehicle. They raced across the field, Aiden tugging Danny along. Only a few steps separated them from the safety of the van when Aiden cried out in pain, his back arching, and dropped Danny's hand. Bright red blossomed over the back of his shoulder as he fell to his knees. Danny knelt next to him, pressing his hand to the wound.

"Come on, Aiden, we're almost there. Help me get you into the van. Then I can tend to your shoulder. You're going to be fine. We just need to get to safety and get some pressure on that wound."

Aiden groaned in pain, but he tried to push himself to his feet. A bullet slammed into the side of the van above their heads. Danny threw himself over Aiden, flattening them both to the ground. He glanced back over his shoulder to see Melissa walking toward them, firing her weapon. She aimed straight at Danny and Aiden but didn't seem to care who she hit in her march through the chaos. Shit. Danny snatched the keys from Aiden's hand even as he searched for a weapon. Nothing. All of the guns were back in the middle of the field, scattered among the bodies of the dead and unconscious.

"Kier!" he shouted, then covered his head with his arms even as he blanketed Aiden's back.

Alex shouted her brother's name a second before a huge explosion rocked the ground. The top floor of the compound erupted. Chunks of building went flying high into the air and rained down on them as a large section of wall tumbled down to land on most of the combatants. A wave of hot air slammed into Danny, followed by tiny bits of cement and glass that pelted him, leaving bruises and abrasions in their wake. The noise seemed to go on forever before giving way to silence and stillness.

Danny lifted his head, throat closing. He forced himself to turn his head toward the disaster. He sucked in a long slow breath, then opened his eyes. He clapped a hand to his mouth to keep from getting sick. Flames still danced in the upper level of the building, which looked as though something had taken a bite out of it with long, sharp teeth. Embers floated up into the sky and drifted down toward them. The field, once the scene of a fierce battle, now contained piles of rubble, twisted metal, and other burned debris. Nothing stirred. Nothing made a sound.

He eased himself off Aiden, then laid a hand on his back.

Aiden turned his head and glanced up at him.

"Oh, thank God. Are you okay?"

He nodded. "I'm fine. What about the others? Where's Alex?"

"Take a look." Danny gestured to the disaster area behind them.

Aiden's eyes went wide, and he pushed to his feet with a wince.

"Careful. Your shoulder?"

"The shoulder's still sore, but the bleeding has slowed. Regardless, we've got work to do."

The two started toward the debris field. "Alex! Kier!"

Again, silence greeted them.

"Where's the last place you saw them before the explosion?"

"I think I saw Kier over there." Danny pointed to a spot in the middle of the grounds and rushed for it, calling for Kier as he ran.

When Danny reached his destination, he looked around for any sign of Kier but found nothing. He started grabbing chunks of rock and heaving them aside, determined to clear the whole damn area of every piece of wreckage if that's what it took.

A section of the rock started moving. Danny rushed toward it, but before he got there, a piece of Sheetrock flipped over, freeing the person beneath. Kier rose to his feet, brushing the dust and dirt off himself. Tears burned in Danny's eyes at the sight of the man he cared so much about standing before him alive, if battered. He rushed to him and flung his arms around him, burying his face in Kier's shoulder.

"Oh God. I was so scared."

Kier squeezed him back. "I'm fine."

"You're not fine." Danny ran his hands over Kier, assessing every cut and bruise.

"Then let's say I was lucky. No major injuries. I was more concerned about you. When I saw her shooting at you— Did you get hit?" Kier cupped Danny's face.

"I'm fine. Aiden was shot in the shoulder, but he's healing already. We need to find Alex and get the hell out of here."

Danny held him tight once more, then stepped away and turned to seek out Aiden.

"Get this fucking thing off me," Alex groused from under a mound of crumbled cinder block. Aiden rushed to her and helped clear the rubble off her. "That bitch shot me. Is she in here somewhere? Because I'd like to dig her up and kick her ass. Ow. Fuck!" She almost collapsed when she took her first step.

Kier and Danny rushed over. Aiden caught his sister around the waist. "What's wrong?" He looked her over, searching for obvious injury.

"I hurt my damn knee and ankle when the building landed on me."

Kier took Alex's hand and gave it a squeeze. Aiden hugged her until she started grumbling and complaining.

After a few more minutes of digging, they located Rogan still unconscious with a trail of blood oozing from somewhere in his dark hair and his arm lying at an unnatural angle. "We need to get him to a hospital. Rogan put himself on the line for us. We all own him more than one," Kier said.

They located a long flat piece of wood and eased Rogan onto it. Then, being as gentle as possible, they picked their way across the carnage to their van, carrying Rogan on the makeshift stretcher.

"Let's get out of here. Someone call Sharon and tell her she's about to get very busy. First stop, though, St. Michael's ER." Kier eased Rogan down on the rear bench seat, and everyone else piled in after.

Danny scanned the field, looking for other signs of life. "Did anyone see what happened to Melissa?"

"I lost track of her when the building blew. I'm assuming she's still in that field under a mountain of rock and metal."

"If she is, getting crushed by her own building couldn't have happened to a better person."

WARM WATER poured over Danny's head as he stood in the shower in Dr. Sharon's guest bedroom. They'd shown up at her house a bit before sunrise. The poor woman had been at a loss for words after they'd shared the story of the events of the last forty-eight hours. As they'd related their tale to her, she'd seen to their injuries and found places for all of them to sleep. Aiden got the brunt of her attention after everything he'd gone through, much to his chagrin.

After a cursory examination, Danny insisted on a shower before she started poking and prodding him again. The weird side effects of whatever Lydecker had injected into him had subsided by the time they got to Sharon's house, so he'd convinced her that he needed to wash off the blood, grime, and terror of the last day before he could be a cooperative patient. Even more, he needed to steam away the fear of the last week, the attack, being wanted by Purity, all of it. With the death of Dr. Lydecker and the destruction of his notes and samples, the target on his back lessened. But it didn't solve everything. He still needed answers about his blood anomaly and what additional damage, if any, Lydecker's injection caused. Then there was Melissa Moran. No telling if she'd survived the explosion at Purity or not. The thought that she could still be out there somewhere had his stomach clenching. He braced his hands against the tile wall and just breathed. God, he wanted to sleep for a week.

The glass door to the shower stall opened, and warm strong arms wrapped around him. Danny leaned back onto Kier's embrace.

"Hanging in there?" Kier pressed a kiss to his temple.

"I'm managing." Danny reached up and threaded his fingers into Kier's hair. Danny smiled as Kier's hand slid up his chest to rest over his heart. He breathed in Kier's earthy scent. So much had changed in the short time since this whole ordeal started. He couldn't believe all they'd gone through to get to this point, but he'd never regret it. He'd always be grateful for his second chance with Kier.

"I was so damn scared. Scared of what they'd do to you and scared that I wouldn't get to you in time."

"I was terrified, but I never doubted for a minute that you'd get to me. A part of me knew you were coming for me. I kept mentally telling you to hurry your ass up. I could have stood for you to get there a little sooner. I think at some point he was going to start cutting things open, and I'm not sure he planned to use any anesthetic."

"He's gone. Let's not think about it anymore." Kier tightened his embrace and buried his face in Danny's neck for a long moment. Then he trailed kisses down his neck and along Danny's shoulder, making him shiver as they sent tiny shock waves of sensation through his body.

Danny turned in his arms and captured his lips in a slow deep kiss that ended with a shaky breath. He rested his forehead against Kier's and eased his hands over the warm, firm muscle of his chest and down his sides to rest on his hips.

"Scared me when you ran out there to face all those soldiers. I realize that you're stronger and faster and whatnot, but still you could have been shot or worse, killed. Don't know what I would have done if I'd lost you."

Kier ran his fingers over Danny's lips. "I'm fine. Rapid healing is one of the perks of being a vampire. I barely got scratched, although having a building land on me hurt a little." Kier smiled and gave Danny a quick kiss.

"I'm glad Alex and Aiden are okay. How is Aiden?"

"Sharon just finished with him before I came in here. He's going to be fine. He's going to need time to rest and recharge both physically and mentally. What that woman put him through...." Kier shook his head. "Rogan's going to need some time to heal as well. Between the head wound and the broken bones, it's going to be a while before he's back on his feet. Sharon's going to go to the hospital and check on him, keep tabs on his care. The man put it all on the line to help us, so I owe him. I'll help him out how I can."

"It's over, right?"

"For now it seems to be."

Danny leaned back and looked up into Kier's eyes. "You think they're still going to come after me?"

"Don't know. So far we haven't heard anything about Melissa, but Purity has a long way to go on the cleanup."

Danny wrapped his arms around Kier, pulled him close until they were pressed body to body. He wanted to immerse himself in Kier, just let the man take him over and surround him like a safe, sexy blanket. He buried his face in the curve of Kier's neck, pressing his lips to the pulse there, nuzzling in. "I want all the crazy to be over."

"We're working on that. I think now we can put all of our focus on fixing you. After we've rested. Sharon's been going through the information Rogan gave us. She wants to talk after we've *rested*." Kier gave him a slow, sexy smile.

Desire flared to life, sending heat rushing through his body. Danny leaned in and pressed a kiss to Kier's chest. He ran his tongue up to swirl in the dip at the base of his neck. Kier tilted his head back to give Danny better access.

"I love the taste of you. I love the way you feel pressed against me."

Kier cupped his hand around Danny's neck and pulled him up into a breath-stealing kiss. They licked and nipped at each other's mouths, reveling at being alive and together. The kiss ended when Danny's need for air became critical, but they didn't part. Their lips brushed, hands explored, leaving sparks of electricity in their wake.

"I've been thinking."

"That's never good." Kier smiled

Danny rolled his eyes. "You're not funny. Anyway, I've been thinking that regardless of what the blood test results or what Lydecker's notes say, I'd still like you to turn me."

Kier pulled back, eyes locking with Danny's. "We can wait a bit longer. Sharon has the drive with all of Lydecker's notes. She may be able to formulate a treatment, if not a cure, that will allow you to be turned when you're ready. If you're ever ready. I don't want you to ever regret—"

Danny laid a finger over Kier's lips. "Listen. I've been walking the line between vampire and human. I've been turned into a madman's personal lab rat. People may still want to perform tests on me if I'm cured, hell, especially if I'm cured. I'm tired of being stuck in this limbo. I want to live my life." He looked into Kier's ice-blue eyes, brushed his fingers along the strong line of Kier's jaw. "But most important of all, I want to be with you. I want to have a life with you."

Kier cupped Danny's cheek. "You don't have to be like me to have a life with me."

"Kier, you're almost one hundred and fifty years old with a lot of years ahead of you. I won't make you watch me grow old and die. I won't leave you like that. This is it for me. You're it. I want to be with you for as long as you'll have me."

"Are you sure?" Kier searched Danny's eyes.

Danny looked at Kier with as much love and desire as he could muster. Then he wrapped his arms around Kier's neck. "I love you. I loved you then, and I never stopped. I made a mistake when I left you and will be forever sorry about hurting you. If you'll let me, I want to make it up to you. I want to love you forever."

Kier closed his eyes, and a breath shuddered out of him. "I love you too, but I need you to be damn sure about this. It will kill me if I turn you and you hate me for it."

Danny brushed his lips over Kier's. "Never."

"When do you want to do this?"

"Anything wrong with now? I want your blood flowing through me."

Kier barked out a laugh. "How about we let Sharon look you over first." He linked their fingers. "Then I think you need to call your family. After what your brother went through, I think you need to tell them about your decision. After that, I would love to make you mine forever."

SHARON LED Kier and Danny into her lab. A much as Kier loved Sharon, he would be happy to never see the inside of this room again. Just like before, they approached a lab table filled with multiple microscopes, test tube racks, and all manner of scientific machinery.

Sharon sat on a tall stool and flipped open her laptop. Then she looked at Kier and Danny with a sympathetic smile. "Well, gentlemen, I have some news for you."

"I'm guessing it's not good news." Danny leaned into Kier, who laid a hand on the small of his back.

"Well, I guess that all depends on your perspective." She tapped one of the microscopes. "From what I can tell, whatever you were injected with last night, while having a multitude of particularly nasty side effects, did nothing to affect the state of your blood anomaly. If that serum—" She made air quotes with her fingers. "—was supposed to be a cure for vampirism, they were way off the mark."

"Are you sure?" asked Kier, then looked at Danny, who furrowed his brow. "If it wasn't a cure, then what is all that research on his computer?"

"I think Lydecker genuinely thought he was on the road to a cure. His notes track the various experiments that he performed on his son, which resulted in a handful of mutations to his son's cells. These mutations created more aggressive cells, meaning a partial change can occur from ingestion of smaller quantities of blood, but they are also faulty cells. They can't complete the job, so to speak. In his son's case, he was a full vampire before the experimentation began, which leads me to believe that once the vampire blood takes over, there's no changing back."

"So what does that mean for me?"

"Well, it means that if you do nothing, you're going to have episodes more frequently. But since this process can't turn you, eventually your body will shut down."

Kier went cold at her words. She'd told them some of this before, but hearing it now, knowing that the cure didn't exist, made it even worse. He pulled Danny closer and asked, "Are you saying there's nothing we can do to stop this?"

"That's not what I'm saying at all. I'm just not sure Danny is going to like it."

Danny stiffened in his arms. "Why not? What do I have to do?"

Sharon rose and laid a hand on Danny's shoulder. "You're going to have to be turned. Stronger healthy vampire blood cells should help your body complete the process and stop the degenerative process of the flawed cells. You'll be attack-free, but you'll be a full vampire."

"It's safe for Kier to take my blood?"

Sharon smiled. "Based upon my own experiments and what I've gleaned from Lydecker's notes, it should be safe. When I mixed the blood samples I obtained from you and Kier, Kier's healthy cells started converting yours into normal vampire cells. That crazy old bastard Lydecker was so obsessed with finding a cure he overlooked one big fact. At the end of the day, normal vampire cells are hearty, dominant cells. If he'd ever bothered to feed his son regular vampire blood, that would have reversed all of the changes that the genetic tinkering caused."

"So why did I start converting?"

"I just told you, because vampire blood is hearty and dominant. The one thing that Purity's experiments did was somehow make it easier for a human to become a vampire. It significantly decreased the amount of blood needed to get the process rolling. Okay?" She reached out and squeezed Danny's shoulder.

"Okay." That's all Danny said.

Kier had to clear his throat before he could speak again. "Thanks, Sharon. I appreciate everything you've done."

"No, thank you. That information you brought me, even though it couldn't help Danny, may prove useful in other ways. Lydecker's work may have other useful applications. It's actually given me some ideas for some of my own research. But enough of that. I think you two have a few things you need to discuss, and I've got a few patients to attend to upstairs."

They followed her out of the lab and back into her living room. "Lock up on your way out. I'll see you later, boys." Sharon smiled. "By the way, it's nice to see you two are working it out."

"Thanks again, Sharon."

She waved at them, then climbed the spiral staircase to her offices and disappeared through the heavy metal door.

Kier turned to Danny and laid his hands on his shoulders. "You still doing okay with everything? No second thoughts?"

Danny lifted his gaze to Kier's. He smiled, but Kier also saw notes of anger and sadness. "I haven't changed my mind at all. I just can't believe everything we've gone through only to find out that the damn cure never existed. That we were put through all of this fear and worry for nothing."

Kier took Danny's hands in his. "It wasn't for nothing. It brought us back together, and for that I'll never regret anything that happened from the moment you walked back into my bar."

Danny linked their fingers, curling them down to squeeze Kier's hands. "I could have done without the sickness and the pain, but otherwise ditto."

Kier glanced down at the floor. "There's one last thing I need to tell you. Once we do this—once I turn you—we will be connected forever. If we ever break up—"

Danny stepped closer and stopped Kier's words by kissing him. "We won't." Danny tugged Kier toward the door. "Come on. I have a phone call to make, and then we need to work on our forever."

# CHAPTER 14

"I'M NERVOUS." Danny stood in the doorway of Kier's home office while he got the computer set up to make a Skype call to his family. He rubbed palms gone damp on his jeans as he waited.

"They love you, Dan. They need to know what's been happening to you. What's about to happen." Kier rose from the desk chair and held it out for Danny. "Sit. The computer is all set, and you'll feel better once you get through this."

Danny nodded and sat but grabbed Kier's hand so he couldn't leave the room.

Kier gave him a reassuring squeeze, then clicked the mouse to initiate the call.

When the call connected, a pretty dark-haired older woman appeared on the screen. "Danny! Where have you been? I haven't heard from you in days and I was starting to get worried."

"Hey, Ma. I'm okay, but I've gotta tell you it's been— Well, it's been a week. Hey, are Dad and Kev there? I'd like to talk to all of you together."

"Sure, sweetheart, give me a second." Danny's mother disappeared off the screen, but they heard her calling for Alan and Kevin to come in. Danny chuckled even as he wiped his palm again. He'd heard the bellowed summons frequently while growing up.

Once Danny's family all crowded around the computer, he started in on his story. "The first thing I need you to know is that about a week ago I was attacked by a vampire when leaving work." Danny's family emitted a collective cry of distress, then all began talking at once. "Guys, please. I'm going to be fine. There are going to be a lot of, well, changes in my life."

"Oh honey, why didn't you call us? We could have come taken care of you."

"I was being taken care of, Mom. Everyone, I'd like you to meet Kieran McCade. He's the man I love, the man who saved my life, and—" His stomach churned. "—he's a vampire."

The room went silent, but that wouldn't last long. Danny's words had been the verbal equivalent of lighting a fuse on a stick of dynamite. The explosion would come any second now. Sure enough. Danny's parents and brother exploded all at once.

Kier pulled up a chair next to him and took his hand again. Danny looked at him, offered a smile of thanks, and dove into the fray.

An hour later, they disconnected the call and Danny sprawled in his seat, the weight of the conversation he'd just had lying heavy on him. He rolled his head and looked up at Kier.

"Well, that could have gone better. It could have gone worse."

Kier reached out and brushed hair back from Danny's forehead. "Give them time. You threw a lot at them at once. It's going to take some time to process it all."

"I know." Danny rose. "I'm also not missing the irony of defending a man I once ran away from to my family."

Kier stood and pulled him close, wrapping him in a hug.

"Thank you for being here. For letting me handle it all."

"No thanks needed. Caring and support are all part of the deal."

Danny wound his arms around Kier's neck, drew his lips along his jaw, and pressed a soft kiss behind his ear.

Kier shivered even as he began kissing the length of Danny's neck.

A breath huffed out of Danny as electricity danced along his skin and his breathing picked up speed. "If you're trying to make me forget about that call, it's working." Danny smiled and tilted his head. He slid his hands up Kier's flank and make slow sweeps over Kier's back.

When Kier found that one spot on his neck that could drive him out of his mind, he exploited the weakness, kissing and sucking until he made Danny moan. Danny needed to touch. He needed Kier's body under his hand, pressed tight against him. He reached for the hem of Kier's shirt, but Kier stepped just out of reach. Danny gasped out his denial at the loss of contact.

"Let's move this elsewhere." Kier took Danny's hand and led him into the bedroom. He flipped back the covers on the wide bed and then pulled Danny close.

"Do you know what's about to happen?"

"Just the basics. It's blood exchange between the two of us, and then I'll… change."

Kier nodded.

"Will it hurt?"

A wide, sexy smiled spread over Kier's face. "Love, I promise you you'll feel nothing but pleasure every step of the way." Kier leaned until his lips brushed Danny's. "Are you ready?"

"Yes. I love you and I want this. Anomaly or no anomaly, this is my choice. You are my choice."

Kier smiled, the look so full of love and longing it took Danny's breath away. Then Kier leaned in and took Danny's mouth in a kiss that made every thought and worry float out of his head and lights dance behind his eyes.

This time when Danny reached for the hem of his shirt, Kier didn't stop him from lifting it up and off. Kier made quick work of Danny's shirt in turn.

Kier trailed kisses along Danny's cheek, his jaw, down his throat. Danny's lips parted. He gasped at the jolt of sensation those soft touches sent through him. He moved on to the pulse in his neck, placing a kiss there before licking downward to kiss the hollow at the base of his throat. Heat unfurled deep inside Danny, wound its way through his system. His skin tingled everywhere Kier touched and tasted him. Danny gasped out Kier's name when he slid his hands up Danny's chest and circled a nipple.

"Like that, love? We're just getting started."

"I need to lie down. You're going to kill me." They made quick work of the rest of their clothes. Then Kier eased him down onto the bed.

Kier leaned over him, a wicked smile on his face, before he lowered himself to lick and suck at Danny's nipples.

Danny jerked under his skillful mouth. He stroked Kier's hair, relishing the sensation of the smooth silken strands sliding between his fingers. He clutched the solid muscle of Kier's shoulders as Kier used his teeth on him. He couldn't stop a low moan from escaping. Heat spread, and his body pulsed and hardened as Kier continued his downward explorations.

Kier bypassed the part of him that wanted immediate attention. Instead he caressed Danny's calves and worked his way up to his thighs.

"I need you. Need to touch you."

"Soon, love. Just enjoy for now." He slid his hand up Danny's thigh. Danny splayed his legs, giving Kier access to nip and suck his way up Danny's inner thighs. Kier licked the crease of his groin and pressed a quick kiss to his cock before moving back up.

"Oh, you bastard. You're going to pay for that." Danny dragged Kier up and claimed his mouth. Kier chuckled as he dove into the kiss. Danny cupped Kier's ass with both hands and pulled Kier tight against him as he ground their cocks together, needing the delicious skin-on-skin friction. He reveled in the sexy rumbles that rolled out of Kier, the hot breath and warm wet mouth against his overheated flesh.

Danny's hands never stopped moving, touching, finding all the places that made Kier moan and gasp. God, those sounds. Everything about this man drove Danny out of his mind. He licked the sheen of salty sweat from Kier's neck and sucked at the pulse point, wanting to mark him, claim him as his own just as Kier would claim him.

Kier growled, then eased away from Danny. He rolled toward the nightstand, tugged open the drawer, and retrieved a bottle of lube.

"Now, where was I? Oh yeah." He licked Danny's hard nipple again. He swirled his tongue around then over the firm point. Danny hissed and gasped. Chest heaving, Danny reached up to squeeze the other neglected nipple, but Kier batted his hand away and replaced Danny's fingers with his. He squeezed and fire flashed through Danny. He cried out, arching up. He couldn't think, only feel as his entire body throbbed with the exquisite pleasure.

Kier hummed and a sexy little grin spread over his face. "So sensitive. I love how you respond to me."

Danny shivered as Kier's hot breath wafted over his damp skin. Those wicked fingers skimmed down Danny's body, dancing and dipping over and into his belly button. Kier chuckled as the muscles of Danny's stomach quivered and clenched under his teasing fingers and tongue. Kier's eyes met Danny's, then dilated so wide only a thin ring of icy blue showed around the dark pupil. His lips parted and his tongue darted out to lick his lips.

"My God, you're beautiful." Danny carded his fingers through Kier's hair.

"So are you, my love. So are you." He leaned in and pressed openmouthed kisses over the length of Danny's cock. Danny couldn't hold back the sounds that Kier forced from him with his skilled touch. Kier played his body like a master. Again Danny cried out when Kier took him into his mouth. He swallowed him deep, all but making his eyes cross.

"Fuck, Kier. Fuck."

He released him long enough to reply, "We're getting there."

Danny glanced at Kier's eyes and noted the red glow shining in their depths. "You are so fucking beautiful."

Kier sucked him back into his mouth, and with every suck, every lick, he worked to coax out every ounce of pleasure. Danny's heart hammered, his breathing rapid, making him light-headed.

"I need more." Danny fisted his hand in Kier's hair and pumped his hips. Kier moaned, and the vibration against his cock made Danny's brain short-circuit. Wave after wave of electricity coursed through his body, building, building until Kier gripped his hips and with a final lick of the head of his cock, pulled off.

"Oh, you fucking suck!" Danny slammed his hand against the mattress.

"I do and quite well, but we're nowhere near done yet."

Kier shoved at his knees. Danny let them fall to his sides. Kier crawled between them and leaned down to place a kiss in the center of Danny's chest. Then he snatched up the bottle of lube, poured some on his fingers. Their gazes stayed locked as Kier eased a slick finger into Danny. Kier started a slow gentle rhythm, pumping in and out as he stroked his other hand over Danny's stomach, his inner thigh. He caressed his sac and the taut skin behind it. Then he paused, and Danny threw back his head, mouth open, breath rasping out. He added a second finger, sending laser bursts of heat firing through him. Kier's skilled fingers caused a delicious stretch and burn. The man stroked him inside and out. Nothing could compete with the amazing sensation of being loved by Kieran McCade. When he added a third finger Danny lost his mind, especially when he curved his fingers and stroked that place inside that made fireworks explode behind his eyes.

Kier eased his hand out, poured a little more lube, and spread it over his cock. Then he lay over Danny. "Ready for me, love?"

Danny kissed him and hitched a leg over Kier's hip. Kier lined himself up with Danny's entrance and eased in.

Danny's eyes went wide as sparks shot through him.

"Talk to me. Tell me what you're feeling."

"More. I need more." Danny clasped at Kier's shoulders as he continued to push into Danny's body, slow and easy until he couldn't go any farther. They lay connected, tasting each other, hands moving and caressing nonstop. Need built in Danny until he couldn't take it anymore. "Move. I need you to move. Please." He met Kier's eyes and wrapped arms and legs around him.

Kier nodded and started a slow, sensual pace. Their eyes stayed locked. Kier's mouth hovered over his, his warm breath tickling Danny's lips with each inward thrust. "You feel amazing. I could spend eternity lying here with you. Inside you." Danny lifted his lips and met Kier's in a kiss so achingly tender it made his throat tighten and tears burn behind his eyes. How he ever thought his life would be better without this man in it, he'd never know.

Kier shifted, hooked an elbow under Danny's knee. He slid in deeper and brushed Danny's prostate with every stroke. Danny cried out as lightning bolts zapped through him, drove him high and higher. Danny fisted his hand in the sheets, needing something, anything to ground him. To keep him from flying out of his body.

"Kier."

"I'm right here, love." He growled the words in Danny's ear.

"Kier!" Danny could only manage that one word as Kier continued to drive into him.

Something warm and wet brushed over his mouth. "Drink, love." Kier pressed his bloodied wrist to Danny's mouth. He latched on to Kier licking and sucking, taking another part of his lover into his body.

When he'd taken enough, Kier pulled away, then took Danny in hand. He thrust and stroked in counterpoint, driving Danny to the brink of pleasure and madness. A ball of energy formed at Danny's core, growing and pulsing, sending blasts of energy through him, making every inch of skin tingle and hum. Before this new sensation could completely consume him, Kier's low, commanding voice snagged his attention and shot him right back up to the edge.

"Danny, you with me?"

Danny nodded as Kier thrust once, twice. "I want you come for me, Danny. Are you ready?" He slammed into Danny again, stoking the fire building deep inside. "I want you to come for me, Danny." He thrust hard one more time, then roared. "Now." He bit hard where Danny's shoulder met his neck, drinking deeply. Danny screamed. Sensation rioted through him as he fell into an orgasmic meltdown. His body bucked and shuddered. Kier pumped his own molten release into Danny as he drank.

Danny began to float; his brain couldn't form a coherent thought if he needed to, and his limbs turned to lead. Drained but euphoric, he fell into darkness and let Kier's blood finish in pleasure what had been started in fear.

THE INCESSANT ringing of his cell phone dragged Kier awake. His internal clock told him the sun hadn't set yet, and the display on his alarm clock confirmed it. He smiled down at Danny, still asleep in his arms. He wanted to close his eyes and slip back into sleep, warm and comfortable, wrapped up with his lover. Not twenty seconds after his phone stopped, it started ringing again.

Kier rolled his eyes at the persistent caller, eased himself out of bed, and padded barefoot into the office where he'd left his phone two days ago. Snatching up his phone, he answered the call.

"Morning, Sharon." He dropped into the desk chair.

"It's about damn time you answered the phone."

"I was a little busy sleeping. I've had an eventful few days." He scrubbed a hand down his face.

"Yeah, I'll bet." He could hear the smirk in her tone.

"Yeah, yeah, you're not funny. So, what's so important?"

"Wanted to let you know that I've gotten word that Melissa Moran has gone missing."

Kier sat up straight. "Where'd you hear that? How is that even possible? Chunks of that building landed on all of us."

"I've got a friend at the local hospital and another with the Sinclair Fire Company. They've combed through the rubble, and they believe pulled out everyone they can find. Twenty-five people are accounted for. From what you told me, Melissa would have made twenty-six on Purity's side. They've thoroughly searched the area and there is no sign of her, living or dead."

"Well, shit." Kier paused and dragged a hand through his hair. "Have you told Aiden or Rogan yet?"

"I told Aiden first, as soon as I got word."

"How'd he take it?"

"I suspect he's more disturbed by the news than he's letting on. He said something about wanting to take a real vacation this time and get out of town for a while. I offered him my vacation home in the mountains. I think he's going to take me up on it. Poor boy needs a break. He needs to rest and feed and heal."

"How about Rogan?"

"Poor guy is a little worse for wear, but he'll be all right. He's not a happy camper. He tried to drag his broken behind out of his hospital bed so he could go get his brother."

"Tell him to stay put. I'm going to send someone to pick up his brother and take him to see Rogan."

"I'll find them someplace safe to stay while he's getting back on his feet. Likely, I'll put them up in one of my properties. This way I can keep an eye on them. It's the least I can do. I owe Rogan big."

"I'll let him know you said that. It should settle him down. Stubborn man. A head injury and broken bones and he wants to go gallivanting off to play hero." She snorted in disgust. Kier just smiled.

"How's Danny holding up?" Kier could hear the sly smile in Sharon's voice.

"He's doing better than I expected."

"No complications with the turning?"

"Not so far. He's come through beautifully. I still can't believe it. I never thought this day would come. Hell, I never expected to see him again. Now, he's mine. It's a little surreal."

A long silence stretched between them. "Well, it's about damn time. It was only a matter of time before you both pulled your heads out of your asses and fixed what was broken between you two."

Kier laughed. "I don't know what to say to that. Thank you for everything, Sharon. We wouldn't have survived this without your help."

"Yeah, yeah. Go kiss your man and get started on that life you've been waiting so long to begin. I'll call you later." She hung up before he could say goodbye.

"I think I'll go do that." He smiled. Warmth spread through him at the thought of kissing Danny awake. He thought about all they'd been through to get to this point. Pain or pleasure, he wouldn't change it.

Kier stood and headed back to the bedroom. Danny still lay in bed, a rumpled sexy mess. He lay on his back, lips parted, sheet tangled around his waist, exposing smooth chest and flat stomach. Need flared to life in Kier. He wanted to kiss every inch of Danny's soft skin. As heat wound its way through him, he couldn't think of a single reason to resist temptation.

He crossed to the bed, sat, then leaned over to lick and bite a hardened nipple.

Danny woke with a moan and arched into Kier's mouth as his slid his fingers into Kier's hair.

He kissed his way up Danny's chest and neck, then claimed his mouth.

"Hey." Danny pulled Kier close and wrapped his arms around him.

Kier smiled at him. "Hey yourself. How are you feeling?"

"Like hell and never better all at once. How long have I been out?"

"You've been in and out for about two days, and it's not surprising you'd feel a little ragged. The body goes through a lot when you turn. When you add in everything that's happened lately, you've been through more than most."

Kier leaned down and brushed soft, drugging kisses over Danny's lips. Danny cupped the back of his head and took the kiss deeper, mating their mouths until they were both breathing hard.

Kier couldn't stop the smile if he tried. "What was that for?"

"Lots of reasons. Because I'm glad we're both alive, because I'm glad I have you here in my arms… because I love you."

"I love you too. I love that I'll have you with me for eternity." Kier stared into Danny's warm chocolate eyes. Happiness radiated from him, but Kier couldn't help asking just one more time. "Still no regrets, right? I mean, there's no going back now, but I just want to make sure I'm not going to spend the next few centuries with a moody, self-loathing vampire."

With a laugh, Danny threw his arms around Kier and held him close. He eased away, but his hands continued stroking Kier's back in soothing circles.

"I made my choice. I chose you and will continue to choose you, for as long as you'll have me. The rest will sort itself out."

A lump formed in Kier's throat. Dammit. He dug for some of his famous stoicism and failed miserably. He wrapped himself around Danny and rocked them both. "I'm being silly, I know, but I never thought we'd get here. Never thought we'd find our way back to each other again. No matter how much I wanted it, if you weren't willing to give me a second chance…."

Danny cupped Kier's cheek. "I was the one who needed forgiving."

Kier shook his head, mirroring the gesture. "Let's just agree that we both screwed up and put it in the past." The hand that Danny laid over Kier's had a fine tremor, and a hint of red glowed deep in his eyes. Someone was hungry. "I think it's time I gave you your first lesson as a full-fledged vampire. It's breakfast time."

Danny turned his head, pressing his lips to Kier's palm. He ran his tongue up Kier's hand until he reached the tip of his middle finger, then sucked it into his mouth. That wicked suction sent heat racing through Kier.

Danny gave him a heavy-lidded look as the red glow grew brighter. *Damn, that's sexy.* He slid his finger out of Danny's mouth as he adjusted himself, then offered him his wrist. He quirked his eyebrow in challenge.

"I'm not sure how to…." Danny stared at it for a moment, then back up at Kier before lowering his mouth.

"Trust your instincts. You know how to do this."

Danny held his gaze for a minute, then glanced down at Kier's wrist. He pulled the offered wrist to his mouth and licked along the path of the radial artery. Then he set his teeth to the skin and eased them into the vessel. Kier moaned. The caress of Danny's lips on his skin and the suction of his mouth reverberated in every part of his body, sending desire pulsing through him to the place that craved Danny's touch. After a minute Danny retracted his fangs and licked Kier's wrist to seal the punctures.

"Knew you'd make an amazing vampire."

Danny smiled and pressed his body to Kier's. He cupped his ass, grinding against him, forcing a hard gust of air from Kier's lungs.

"Now that I've eaten, how about I bring you breakfast in bed."

"Sounds like an excellent idea." Kier stole a kiss, then started to lead Danny back to the bedroom. Danny crowded him from behind and wrapped his arms around Kier's waist.

"One thing, though. From here on out it's you and me, right? I know that we need to feed, and it can't always be just you and me. So, when we need to include another person, promise me we will always do that together."

Kier rolled them over the bed, pinning Danny beneath him. He stared into Danny's eyes, wanting him to see and hear the vow in his words. "Always you and me together. I promise."

The wattage on Danny's smile increased. A lottery winner couldn't be any happier than Kier right at this moment.

"You know, hundreds of years is a long time to spend with one person, but you're stuck with me now."

Kier lowered himself so they lay chest to chest. He kissed him, soft and slow. "Danny Reynolds, I wouldn't want it any other way."

The joy in the smile that spread across Danny's face echoed inside Kier. Kier joined their mouths, losing himself in the man who held his heart and the knowledge that they would be joined for eternity mind, body, and soul.

RAYNA VAUSE is a lifelong learner who wants to live on a Disney cruise ship traveling the world and thinks purple should be considered a natural hair color.

She loves to craft tales full of mystery, magic, and adventure and is a proud geek who injects a little bit of her geeky, tech-obsessed soul into every story. Rayna has collected degrees in English, Computer Information Systems, Radiologic Science, and more are on the way.

She's planned readers' and writers' conferences for the last ten years and has spent years serving on the boards of her various writers' organizations. Rayna is a member of RWA, RRW, and a founding member of Liberty States Fiction Writers.

When she isn't writing, she's likely indulging her love of video games, working through her massive TBR pile, or plotting her next novel. She lives in southern New Jersey, just a bit outside of Philadelphia, and shares a home with her cat, the Princess Muffin.

Website: www.raynavause.com
Facebook: www.facebook.com/raynavauseauthor
Twitter: @Rayna_Vause

DEMON
of MINE

RAYNA VAUSE

Climbing the corporate ladder can be hell....

As a collections demon, Zavier grants his "clients" one wish in exchange for their souls. His job sucks, but once you make a deal with Corporate South, they own you. The trouble is, Zavier's not a very good collections demon, with his tendencies to spurn authority and find loopholes to help deserving clients out of their contracts. He's under scrutiny from the head of his department, who would quite literally like to see him burn. He just needs to close a simple deal to get upper management off his back. Instead, he meets Ryan.

Ryan is desperately searching for a way to save his dying sister. He doesn't believe in magic and demons, but he's out of options. Zavier's not what he expects in a demon, and even more unexpected is the strong sense of familiarity—very intimate familiarity.

While trying to free Ryan from his contract, Zavier discovers secrets unscrupulous even by South standards. Exposing them could cost Zavier everything, but it might be Ryan's only hope.

# www.dreamspinnerpress.com

DREAMSPUN
DESIRES

# EXTRASENSUAL PERCEPTION

## Rayna Vause

*If a stalker doesn't
kill them, the heat
between them might.*

If a stalker doesn't kill them, the heat between them might.

Christopher Vincent is desperate enough for a job that he accepts an offer to entertain as a psychic in a friend's nightclub. Jackson Whitman, one of the club's co-owners, is less than thrilled by the new act. To him, psychics are ridiculous and a liability. But when they come face-to-face, attraction flares to life between them.

Someone is watching Jack and Chris from the shadows. What starts as a series of creepy encounters leads to deadly attacks.

Jack and Chris must set aside their differences and work together to survive a homicidal stalker. But can they survive their explosive connection?

# www.dreamspinnerpress.com

Also from Dreamspinner Press

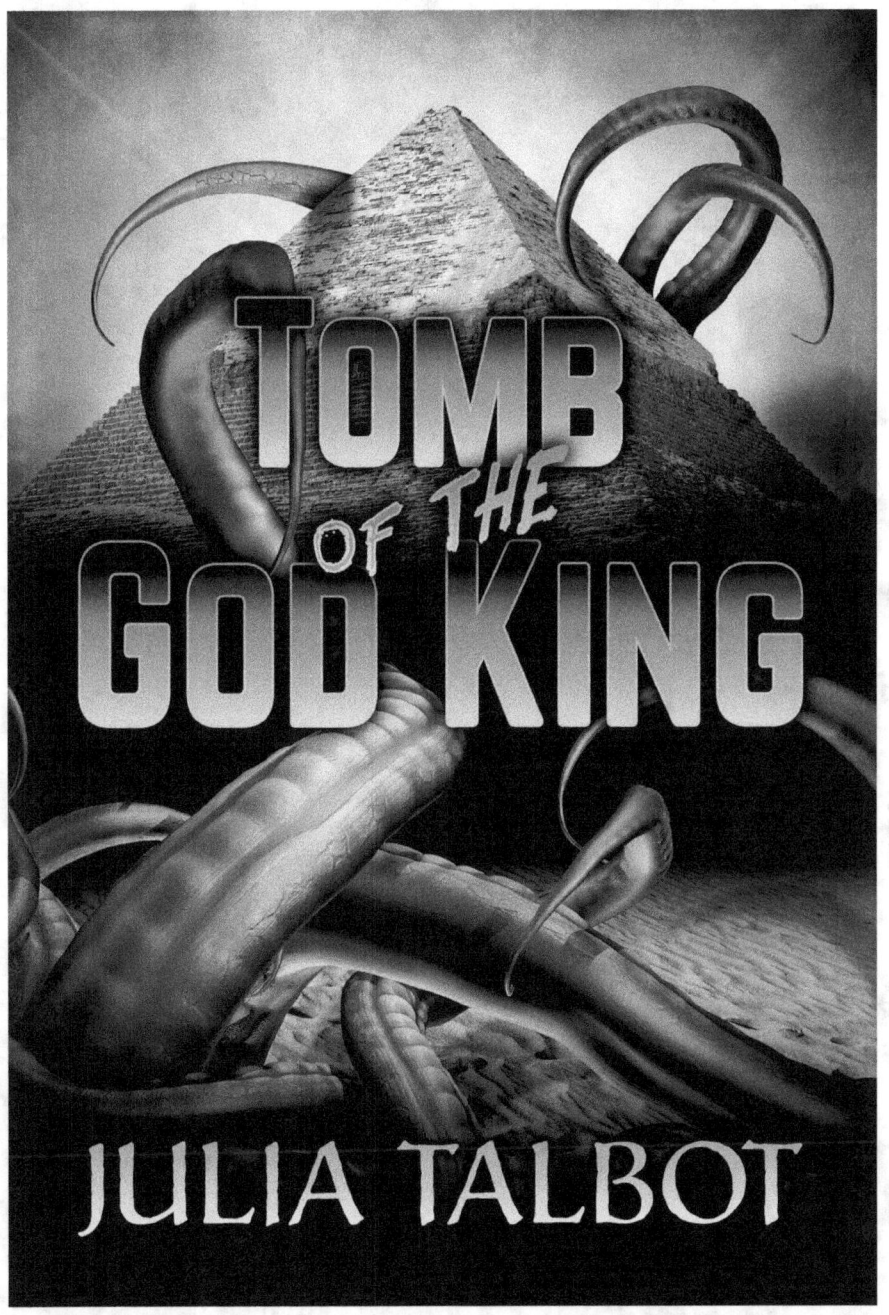

www.dreamspinnerpress.com

www.ingramcontent.com/pod-product-compliance
Lightning Source LLC
Chambersburg PA
CBHW060103260626
47160CB00005B/1778